Frederick Saunders, Frederick Saunders

Character studies

With some Personal Recollections

Frederick Saunders, Frederick Saunders

Character studies
With some Personal Recollections

ISBN/EAN: 9783743389656

Manufactured in Europe, USA, Canada, Australia, Japa

Cover: Foto ©Raphael Reischuk / pixelio.de

Manufactured and distributed by brebook publishing software (www.brebook.com)

Frederick Saunders, Frederick Saunders

Character studies

CHARACTER STUDIES.

CHARACTER STUDIES,

WITH

SOME PERSONAL RECOLLECTIONS.

BY THE AUTHOR OF

"SALAD FOR THE SOLITARY AND THE SOCIAL," "PASTIME
PAPERS," "EVENINGS WITH THE SACRED POETS," "STORY
OF SOME FAMOUS BOOKS," "STRAY LEAVES OF
LITERATURE," ETC.

"*Time, who steals our years away,*
Shall steal our pleasures too,
But memory of the past will stay,
And half our joys renew."

NEW YORK:
THOMAS WHITTAKER, 2 AND 3 BIBLE HOUSE.
1894.

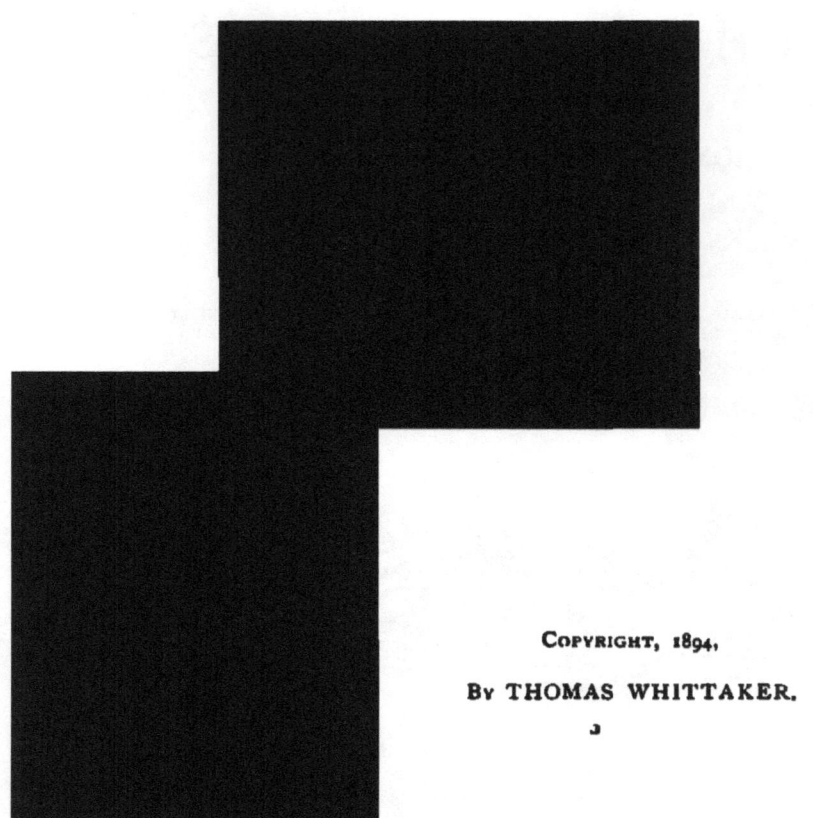

BURR PRINTING HOUSE, NEW YORK.

FORE-WORDS.

IF, with Thackeray, we believe that "memory is part of our souls, and is eternal," then its bright visions may be said to form an essential element of life's best estate, and also to compensate, in some measure, for its gloomy seasons of sorrow and of sadness.

The object of the following pages is to record some pleasant recollections of a privileged friendship or acquaintanceship with certain distinguished personages who have since passed beyond the horizon of time.

> Worthies, alas ! now passed away,
> Whose presence charmed life's earlier day,
> Whose wisdom, culture, courtesy,
> Memory enshrines as legacy.

These memorial sketches do not pretend to complete portraiture ; they are rather quiet studies of characters, eminent alike for their intellectual culture and moral excellence.

We instinctively cherish respect for

persons whose names have become illustrious by their achievements, whether by their inventive genius, their intellectual endowments and culture, as leaders of thought, or by their high moral worth, as elevators of society. In the economic and industrial estimate of its progressive development, the thinker and the doer equally present their respective claims to our regard, each being essentially necessary in promoting the advancement of mankind. There is yet another element, no less requisite to the formation of symmetrical and exalted character in a community—that which is, indeed, the basis of its moral power —its spiritual culture. Wherever this happy combination prevails in a country, the highest expression of individual character also obtains. It is not likely, therefore, that those whose lives have been devoted to the furtherance of such high aims will fail to secure from all true lovers of the race their grateful esteem.   FREDERICK SAUNDERS.

The Astor Library, New York.

CONTENTS.

PAGE

I. EDWARD IRVING : Carlyle's estimate of—The early days of—His *personnel*—His chosen books—His first sermon—His arrival in London—His Caledonian chapel —Coleridge's opinion of him—Crowded audiences—Origin of his great popularity—His new church dedication by Chalmers—His published "Orations"—Address at the Bible Society meeting—"Unknown tongues"— Great missionary discourse—Prophetic discourses—His trial for heresy—Closing days and death.............. 1

II. ANNA JAMESON : Her early history—Travels on the Continent—Her "Diary of an Ennuyée"—Her "Characteristics of Women"—Visit to the United States and Canada—Christian art in the Middle Ages—Her return to Europe—Her efforts in behalf of the elevation of woman—Longfellow's high tribute to her "Sacred and Legendary Art"—Her descriptions of Niagara and elsewhere—Various estimates of her character and genius.. 31

III. WASHINGTON IRVING : Description of his home— Its history, by himself—His first visit to Europe— —Meeting with Roscoe—First meeting with Scott—Visit to Dryburgh and Melrose—His return to New York— His Mission to Madrid—Visit to the Alhambra—His researches for his "Life of Columbus"—His brief dinner speeches — His London publisher, Murray— Meeting the London literary magnates—Scott's friendship—Opinions of the "Sketch-Book" and "Knickerbocker"—Literary party at Sunnyside—His connection with the Astor Library — Subsequent sickness and death—Funeral at Sleepy Hollow Cemetery—Tributes to his memory............................ 65

PAGE

IV. HENRY WADSWORTH LONGFELLOW : The poet in his historic home—Description of it—Genial and generous spirit displayed in referring to his contemporaries—The illustrated edition of his works—Various high opinions of his productions—Origin of some of his poems—Select extracts—His visits abroad—His academic honors—His poem on the flowers............... 113

V. WILLIAM CULLEN BRYANT : As a pastoral and ethical poet—His love of natural objects—His pedigree of Puritan origin and early life—Arrival in New York—His first noteworthy production, " Thanatopsis"—His connection with the *Evening Post*—His home at Roslyn, L. I. —Extracts from his poems—His increasing popularity as a poet—His laborious career as a journalist—His visits abroad—His closing days.......... 133

VI. JOSEPH GREEN COGSWELL : His early history—Graduate of Harvard—His voyage to India—Establishes a high school at Raleigh, N. C.—Visits John Jacob Astor—His establishment of the Public Library—Is appointed librarian—Makes trips to Europe for obtaining books of high repute—The Astor Library is built, and the books, numbering 80,000 volumes, placed on its shelves—First opened to the public—The great art productions exhibited—Excellent skill in selection of its books—His devotion to it of over a score of years—His resignation of his official relations with the Library—Extracts from his later correspondence............... 155

"If we work upon marble, it will perish; if we work upon brass, time will efface it; if we rear temples, they will crumble into dust; if we work upon immortal minds, if we imbue them with principles, with the just fear of God and love of our fellow-men, we engrave on those tablets something which will brighten to all eternity."

DANIEL WEBSTER.

EDWARD IRVING.

Born 1792, died 1834.

" The good man suffers but to gain,
  And every virtue springs from pain,—
  As aromatic plants bestow
  No spicy fragrance while they grow,
  But crushed, or trodden to the ground,
  Diffuse their balmy sweets around."

—GOLDSMITH.

EDWARD IRVING.

"EDWARD IRVING's warfare has closed, if not in victory, yet in invincibility and faithful endurance unto the end. . . . His was the freest, brotherliest, bravest human soul mine ever came in contact with : I call him, on the whole, the best man I have ever (after hard trial enough) found in this world, or now hope to find." Thus wrote Thomas Carlyle concerning the subject of the present sketch, who half a century ago filled so prominent a place in the annals of his day. Such high testimony from such a source must have been of one well worthy of such an eulogy and of our study, for wherever he went men acknowledged the spell of his genius.

Until the appearance of Carlyle's "Reminiscences" comparatively little was known of the real character of the celebrated Scotch minister, Edward Irving.   Mrs. Oliphant's charming memoir of his brilliant and checkered career presents his portraiture in a fuller and more complete manner than any other that had been published.   Since that publication, the Rev. G. Carlyle, Irving's nephew, has given to the world the collective edition of the writings of the renowned preacher, which, forming five large volumes, constitute an enduring monument of his genius and character.

Several years before the publication of the fore mentioned works, the essential part of the present desultory sketch appeared in a New York quarterly.   In that paper the writer, whose acquaintance with Mr. Irving commenced a short time after his arrival in London, gave descriptions and incidents then fresh in his recollection ; and these are incorporated in the present sketch, as they may possibly afford some new glimpses of Mr. Irving's remarkable career.

One of the leading British reviews

some time since remarked that if a "sketch of Edward Irving—as he was in the days of his glory, drawn from memory by a hand at once appreciative and discriminative—could be had, it would be of real interest, as well to the historian as to the divine." It is not to be inferred, however, that the above requisitions are all met in the present paper, which is but an attempt for the most part to present what the writer saw and heard of Mr. Irving when he was in the zenith of his fame.

Reverting back to those days of Irving's wonderful popularity, his brilliant career seems as transient as it was picturesque, heroic, dramatic, and sad ; a life of seeming paradoxes—short, if years are its only measurement, but long and luminous, if computed by great thoughts, feelings, and sorrows.

There was a strange witchery about Edward Irving ; his utterances were fervid and glowing, often stately and Miltonic. He was of commanding stature, of dark and melancholy beauty of

countenance, with a profusion of raven-
black hair parted on the centre of his
head, and flowing down to his shoul-
ders ; with piercing dark eyes, one of
which was oblique—all which produced
a very profound impression. In addition, there seemed to be a weird fascination about his presence—an apparent
austerity, almost suggestive of the as-
ceticism of the cloister, in his public
ministrations ; yet it is well known that
he possessed a heart singularly sensitive
and gentle.

He does not seem to have courted
fame, but rather to have sought to be a
worshipper at the shrine of nature, by
the hill-side or the romantic glens of
his own classic soil, than to pore over
the pages of the collective wisdom of the
past. It is said that, at twelve years of
age, he used to take his solitary ramble
over the wild heather, with only the
Bible under one arm and a loaf of bread
under the other ; and thus would seek,
at their very source, to draw deep wisdom and inspiration alike from the great

statute-books of heaven and of earth. He imbibed the love of liberty with his pure mountain air ; and doubtless at early dawn and dewy eve his impassioned soul was filled with lofty aspirations and earnest yearnings after that higher estate of being which to him seemed so real.

Thus did he commune with the celestial, the ideal, and the real. It is not surprising, therefore, that he should have been moulded after a model dissimilar from that of his contemporaries and his age. Far from disdaining the toils of studious scholarship, however, Irving not only possessed in an eminent degree an acquaintance with the sciences and the general branches of human lore, but he became himself essentially a poet. Mr. Irving took his degree at the University of Edinburgh in 1809, when he attracted the notice of the professors of the classics and mathematics.

He was then forming his taste and style on the model of certain books, which became his prime favorites ;

these were the " Arabian Nights," Ossian's poems (which he is said always to
have carried in his pocket), Homer, and
the works of Hooker. Carlyle has described him as he saw him at this period,
when he returned from the University
of Edinburgh. " We have heard of
famed professors, of high matters, classi-
cal, mathematical—a whole wonderland
of knowledge ; nothing but joy, health,
hopefulness without end looked out
from the blooming young man."

He then, in his eighteenth year, became a teacher in a mathematical school
at Haddington. It is said that often in
moonlit nights he would gather his
pupils about him, when he would recite
passages from Milton's epic or Ossian's
poems, and give to the recital such
dramatic force as almost to frighten his
little flock. Among his scholars at Haddington was his favorite one, Jane Welsh,
who afterward became the wife of his
friend, Thomas Carlyle. In 1815 Irving
delivered his first sermon at Annan,
Scotland ; and the town turned out to

hear him. When he had reached the
middle of his discourse, by some incau-
tious movement of his hand he tilted
aside the Bible and with it the manuscript of his sermon. That direful paper,
which Scotch congregations then held
in " high despite," fluttered down upon
the precentor's desk beneath. Much
excitement prevailed through the assembly, but Irving calmly bent his tall figure over the pulpit, grasped the manuscript as it lay, put it into his pocket,
and continued his discourse as fluently
as before. His success, which gained
by the accident, was triumphant. But
this was not an auspicious time ; as a
preacher he seemed to fail ; and he is
said to have destroyed his sermons.

In his despondency he was contem-
plating a plan of going as a missionary
to the East, " after the apostolic order,
without scrip or purse," when an invitation came to him from Dr. Andrew
Thomson to occupy his pulpit at St.
George's Church, Edinburgh, when Dr.
Chalmers was expected to be present.

This led to his appointment of assistant
to Dr. Chalmers. " I will preach to
them if you think fit," said Irving ;
" but if they bear with my preaching
they will be the first people who have
borne with it." About two years later
came the call to the Caledonian Chapel,
Hatton Garden, London, where some
two or three months sufficed of his eloquent addresses to stir all the British
metropolis with excitement and curiosity, attracting crowded audiences of the
aristocracy and nobility to see and hear
the great Scottish Boanerges. Among
the distinguished persons, scientific,
literary, and social, seen in this obscure
chapel were, Lord Brougham, Sir James
Mackintosh, Wilkie, Canning, the Duke
of York, Coleridge, and Carlyle.

It was about this time that Coleridge
said of him : " I hold that Edward Irving possesses more of the spirit and purposes of the first reformers ; that he
has more of the head and heart, the life
and unction, and the genial power of
Martin Luther than any man of this or

the last century. I see in Edward Irving a minister of Christ after the order
of Paul."

That was the golden period of Irving's career, when he delivered some of
his masterly discourses, and when he
was flushed with the triumphs of his
genius. Those discourses formed the
book which he styled " Orations for the
Oracles of God," of which a leading
contemporary critic thus spoke : " There
is a swelling grandeur in these orations
both of thought and expression, a rich-
ness of conception and grasp of imagination, with a wondrous poetry of spiritual feeling, which captivate and hold
spellbound the reader."

The recollection of Irving's picturesque
appearance on a Sunday, when the chapel
was crowded by notabilities and eager
masses of persons anxious to hear him,
it is not easy to forget. At eleven
o'clock A.M., the hour of public worship,
the church clerk carried the Bible up to
the pulpit, then followed with slow and
stately steps the surpliced orator, Ed-

ward Irving, calm, dignified, and self-possessed, seemingly conscious of his master-power. He commenced the service by an invocation, and then would read with dramatic effect one of the rugged, unmusical Scottish hymns, which was sung by the congregation, led by the precentor, who occupied a seat below the pulpit. The slow singing ends, and we are charmed by the fine voice of Irving—organ-like, full of melody and modulation—as he reads one of the psalms, and then adds, " Let us pray ;" and here especially we felt conscious of being in the presence of a strangely gifted man. The prayer ended, he announced his text and entered upon his theme, and as he became inspired by its unfolding, his enthusiasm and eloquence, sustained by his graceful action, rose to their full height ; so that a visitor for the first time had been heard to exclaim, " If that man be not mad, he must be inspired." So intense was the eagerness of the people of all classes to hear him that it was found

necessary to issue cards of admission
not only to Hatton Garden Chapel, but
also to the new Gothic church in Regent Square, in which he afterward
preached, the dedication services of
which edifice was a proud day for Irving. This beautiful structure was in
part modelled after York Minster Cathedral, and one of its most exquisite fea-
tures was the elaborately carved oak
pulpit, with its rich Gothic canopy. At
this time the name and fame of Thomas
Chalmers was at its meridian, his " As-
tronomical Discourses" having aston-
ished the intellectual world of London
and elsewhere by their brilliancy and
beauty. Such was the intense anxiety,
therefore, to obtain tickets of admission
to the opening services as soon as it was
announced that Chalmers would take
part on the occasion, that the neighboring streets were blocked up with car-
riages, and the crowds of pedestrians
had to be kept back by the police while
the ticket-holders were being first ad-
mitted to the church. The crowded

audience paid dearly for the privilege
of seeing and hearing the two Scottish
magnates, for the services were weari-
somely protracted and fatiguing. Irving commenced the order of procedure
by reading a long chapter from one of the
old prophetical books of the Bible, upon
which he dilated at yet greater length.
Then followed the slow singing of a
hymn, and after this Chalmers arose to
speak from the text.* His broad Scotch
accent was so marked as to make it difficult to catch some of his utterances ;
but as he advanced with his subject his
manner of delivery—which was the op-
posite of Irving's, being heavy and dull
—then became eloquent in diction and
earnest in manner.

The supposed origin of Irving's remarkable popularity was this : Sir James
Mackintosh happened to hear the new
Scotch minister referring in his prayer
to a family of orphans connected with
his congregation as now " thrown upon

---

* Jeremiah 6 : 16.

the fatherhood of God." This phrase struck the mind of the philosopher, and he repeated it to Canning, then the prime minister ; and shortly afterward, in a discussion on church endowments, he referred to Irving and his masterly eloquence, although connected with the poor and obscure chapel at Hatton Garden. Here it was that he laid the foundation of that brilliant yet brief career of popularity the parallel of which is scarcely to be found in the annals of the Church. A contemporary writer thus refers to the elements which combined to make this modern clerical Demosthenes such a marvel : " In these might be seen independence stalking in his stride, intellect enthroned on his brow, imagination dreaming on his lips, physical energy stringing his frame, and athwart the whole a cross-ray from Bedlam shooting in his eye. It was this which excited such curiosity, wonder, awe, rapture, and tears, and made his very enemies, even while abusing, confess his power and tremble in his presence.

It was this that made ladies flock and faint, which divided attention with the theatres, eclipsed the oratory of Parliament, and made such men as Hazlitt protest, on returning, half squeezed to death, from one of his displays, that a monologue from Coleridge or a burst of puns from Lamb were nothing to a sermon from Edward Irving." His manner and voice, as well as his fine physique, contributed to the charm ; his aspect wild yet grave—now symmetrical in repose, anon terrible with excitement or enthusiasm.

Then there was the style, curiously uniting the beauties and faults of a sermon of the seventeenth century with the beauties and blemishes of a parliamentary harangue of the nineteenth ; quaint as Browne, florid as Taylor, and interspersed with patches from the magic robe of Coleridge. Abrupt and startling as were sometimes his transitions from the majestic and the sublime to the commonplace and the colloquial, such was his oratorical adroitness that these defects, which would have been deemed fatal to an ordinary speaker, were regarded, in his instance, but as among the eccentricities of genius.

In fine, his diction was a new dialect for the sacred desk—it was his own ; and consequently even old and familiar truths came from his lip with a fresh-ness and grace that charmed the ear with their persuasiveness and power. Modelled, for the most part, after the seventeenth-century masters in theology, his style became a rich conglomerate of gems from the Elizabethan age of letters—rich in poetic power and imagery and rhetorical pomp. But it must be confessed that Irving had one serious defect—prolixity. At one of the anniversary meetings held at Hackney, near London, he kept the patient audience nearly three hours ; and on another occasion he preached at the Tabernacle, before the missionary meeting, to the same extent. At one of the anniversary celebrations of the British and Foreign Bible Society, held at Free Masons'

Hall, when Wilberforce was among those present, an exciting incident occurred which is still fresh in the memory of the writer.

Many animated addresses had been delivered touching the question of printing the Bible without the Apocrypha. When the debate was at its height, Irving arose and commenced his speech, which was a stream of astonishing eloquence, till at length, beginning to fulminate against his brethren for their combined opposition to his tenets, he was vociferously hissed. The harmony of the meeting was at an end, and in the midst of the direst confusion he roared out, as few if any beside him could have done, " Do you know in what spirit I am come here to speak that you *dare* to put me down ?" His dauntless courage gained for him a fresh silence, and with moderated feelings he was suffered to conclude his remarks.

When he went through his native district of Annandale there was no church edifice found of sufficient size to accommodate the crowds of persons eager to hear him ; and so he preached to them in the open air—the adjacent churches were closed during his appearance among them.

Before presenting some brief extracts from his first published "Orations for the Oracles of God," it should be remembered that much of the witchery and fascinating charm of Irving's oratory was due to his dramatic power and picturesque *personnel ;* and as this is, of course, lost to the mere *reader* of his discourses, it should be duly allowed for in our estimate of his genius and of the man. The following extract is from the exordium to his first oration :

" There was a time when each revelation of the Word of God had an introduction into this earth, which neither permitted men to doubt whence it came nor wherefore it was sent. If, at the giving of each several truth, a star was not lighted up in heaven, as at the birth of the Prince of Truth, there was done upon the earth a wonder to make her children listen to the message of her Maker. The Almighty made bare His arm ; and through mighty acts, shown by His holy servants, gave demonstration of His truth, and found for it a sure place among the other matters of human knowledge and belief. But now the miracles of God have ceased ; and nature, secure and unmolested, is no longer called on for testimonies to her Creator's voice. No burning bush draws the footsteps to His presence-chamber ; no invisible voice holds the ear awake ; no hand cometh forth from the obscure, to write His purposes in letters of flame. The vision is shut, the testimony is sealed, and the word of the Lord is ended ; and this solitary volume is the sum total of all for which the chariot of heaven made so many visits to the earth, and the Son of God Himself tabernacled and dwelt among us. The truth which it contains once dwelt, undivulged, in the bosom of God ; and on coming forth to take its place among things revealed, the heavens and the earth, and nature, through all her chambers, gave it reverent welcome. Beyond what it contains, the mysteries of the future are unknown. To gain it acceptation and currency, the noble company of martyrs testified unto the death ; the general assembly of the first-born in heaven made it the day-star of their hopes, and the pavilion of their peace.

"If you get not the soul's attachments to the world loosened before death, there will ensue such a rending and agony upon your departure as no loss of country, of wife, or children can be compared with ; and if you take not a cool forethought of the future, nor prepare to meet it, there will come such a brood of fears, such a wreck of hopes as no improvident spendthrift ever encountered. O ye sons of men, if these things are so, and ye tread every moment upon the brink of time, and live upon the eve of judgment, what avail your many cares and your unresting occupations ? Will your snug dwellings,

your gay clothing, and your downy beds
give freshness to the stiffened joints or
remove the disease which hath got a
lodgment in your marrow and in your
bones ? Will a crowded board, and the
full flow of jovial mirth, and beauty's
wreathed smile, and beauty's dulcet
voice charm back to a crazy dwelling
the ardors and graces of youth ? Will
yellow gold bribe the tongue of memory and wipe away from the tablets of
the mind the remembrance of former
doings ? Will worldly goods reach up-
ward to heaven and bribe the pen of
the recording angel, that he should can-
cel from God's books all vestige of our
crimes, or abrogate the eternal law by
which sin and sorrow, righteousness and
peace are bound together ?"

The following passage, referring to
the beatitudes of the future life of the
Christian, for the pomp of its rhetoric
and poetic imagery is a fair illustration
of his power :

" Cannot God create another world
many times more fair, and cast over it a

mantle of light many times more lovely, and wash it with purer dew than ever dropped from the eyelids of the morn? Can He not shut up winter in His hoary caverns, or send him howling over other domains? Can He not form the crystal eye more full of sweet sensations, and fill the soul with a richer faculty of conversing with nature than the most gifted poet did ever possess? Think you the creative function of God is exhausted upon this dark and troublous ball of earth; or that this body and soul of human nature are the masterpiece of His architecture? Who knows what new enchantment of melody, what new witchery of speech, what poetry of conception, what variety of design, and what brilliancy of execution He may endow the human faculties withal? in what new graces He may clothe nature, with such various enchantment of hill and dale, woodland, rushing streams, and living fountains; with bowers of bliss, and Sabbath scenes of peace, and a thousand forms of disporting creatures, so as to make all that the world hath beheld to seem like the gross picture with which you catch infants ; and to make the Eastern tale of romances and the most rapt imagination of Eastern poets like the ignorant prattle and rude structures which first delight the nursery, and afterward shame our riper years. . . . Oh, what untried forms of happy being, what cycles of revolving bliss await the just ! Conception cannot reach it, nor experience present materials for the picture of its similitude ; and though thus figured out by the choicest emblems, they do no more represent it than the name of Shepherd does the guardianship of Christ, or the name of Father the love of Almighty God.''

Carlyle said that Irving's head, when '' the fog-Babylon had not obscured it, was of strong, far-reaching insight ;'' and but for his extremely excitable temperament and the strange infatuation of a few of his fanatical friends, Irving might have held long the high position for which his remarkable gifts qualified him. His false step was his endorsing the idea that the gift of tongues, with other primitive endowments of the Church, was still obtainable in answer to prayer. Having been present on several occasions in his Gothic church when this delusion was manifested by the supposed "gifted," the writer, in common with most of the audience, felt the painful conviction that the whole procedure was a fanatic delusion. These hysterical utterances were rightly called "unknown tongues," since they were utterly incoherent and unintelligible to us. But occult as they were to outsiders, the "gifted" circle pretended to give them an interpretation. Sometimes these eccentric and disturbing persons would burst out with shrill, screaming voices during Irving's sermon and put the audience in great confusion. He would then stop speaking, bow his head reverently, and wait until the utterances ceased, which seemed to be the result of sheer 'exhaustion. Irving himself was never known to claim the possession of the gift of tongues ; but that he became a victim of the delusion, and gave to it the force of his great influence, there seems to be no doubt.

Another exciting doctrine, which Irving espoused with no less zeal and earnestness, was that of the near approach of the millennium and the final restoration of the Jews. He even acquired the Spanish language in order that he might translate a Spanish work that had then just appeared on that subject, professedly by a converted Jew—Ben Ezra—on " The Coming of the Messiah."

Irving seems to have been in advance of his age on another doctrine of the Scriptures—the nature of our Lord's humanity—for he strenuously insisted on the peccability of His body ; and yet he maintained that it was immaculate and free from all taint of sin. Remembering how much that subject has been since discussed by our theologians, Irving has done good service to the Church

and the progressive interpretation of the
Bible. But the tenet was too meta-
physical for the Presbytery of Annan in
his day ; and in the year preceding his
last on earth, that council impeached,
tried, and condemned for heresy the
great and gifted seeker after truth.
But such was the decree of the Presbytery ; and in thus deposing Irving from
the ministry, the gates of the beautiful
edifice which his popularity had erected
were now closed against him.

The touching details of his closing
days show that he had lost the strong
leadership of the flock that now followed
him ; and sadness and sorrow accom-
panied him even to the tomb. After his
expulsion from the church in Regent
Square, Irving frequently gathered a
crowd in various open places in the
metropolis, and preached to crowds
from some temporary platform. On
one occasion it rained heavily, and yet
the services continued under cover of
umbrellas.

Mrs. Oliphant speaks touchingly about

the kindly nature of Irving's married relations, and illustrates this by extracts from the " Journal" which he kept during their temporary separation. This record, she thinks, " has no parallel, perhaps, in modern times—a picture so minute, yet so broad ; a self-revelation so entire ; a witness so wonderful of those household loves, deepened by mutual suffering and sorrow, which so far transcends in its gravity and soberness the more voluble passions of youth, has never, so far as I am aware, been given to the world."

Thomas Carlyle's last interview with Edward Irving has been given to us in his " Reminiscences." " Proceeding toward Chelsea," he states, " on a bright May day, I noticed in Kensington Gardens a dark male figure sitting between two white female ones under a tree. The former arose and stalked toward me, whom, seeing it was Irving—but how changed in the two years since I had last seen him. He had suddenly become an old man ; his head, which I had left raven black, was grown gray on the temples, almost stone white. The face was hollow, wrinkly, collapsed ; the figure, still perfectly erect, yet seemed to have lost all its elasticity and strength. He was very kind and loving ; but his tone was low, pensive, and full of sadness.''

The closing scene on earth was nigh —one of touching pathos and sadness ; it occurred at Kirkaldy, the birthplace of his wife. The supreme hour approached when hope of recovery was lost ; he was heard to be murmuring some sonorous syllables to himself ; and as his father-in-law, Rev. Dr. Martin, bent his ear close to him, to his joy he discovered that he was reciting in Hebrew the twenty-third Psalm !

'' As the gloomy December Sabbath sank into the night shadows,'' says his biographer, '' his last audible words on earth fell from his pale lips. The last utterance that could be understood was, ' If I die, I die unto the Lord.' And so at the wintry midnight hour which closed the last Sabbath on earth, the last bonds of mortal trouble dropped asunder, and the saint and martyr entered into the rest of his Lord."

His death excited profound sorrow throughout the religious world ; and most of the clergy of the city and suburbs followed in solemn and sorrowing procession the remains of him whom they so lately excommunicated from their order to his final resting-place, in the crypt of the magnificent cathedral of Glasgow.

Tributes to the exalted character of the subject of this sketch abound ; one or two may suffice :

"No man, no child ever met the warm glance of his eye or heard the kind accents of his blessing but treasured the memory ever afterward. The impulse which he gave to larger views of God's love and deeper faith in the presence and power of His Spirit, which as the result the century has received, cannot well be overestimated."

One of Carlyle's closing sentences reads : "Less mendacious soul of a man than my noble Irving's there could not well be."

ANNA JAMESON.

Born 1797, died 1860.

" To see her kindle into enthusiasm amidst the gorgeous natural beauty, the antique memorials, and the sacred Christian relics of Italy, was a sight which one who witnessed it will never forget. There is not a cypress upon the Roman hills, or a picture in those vast sombre galleries of foreign palaces, or a Catacomb spread out vast and dark under the martyr-churches of the City of the Seven Hills, which is not associated with some vivid flash of her intellect and imagination, and with the dearer recollections of personal kindness."

—B. R. PARKES.

ANNA JAMESON.

AMONG the many distinguished wom-
en who have contributed to shed lustre
on the Victorian epoch by their noble
service in the realm of literature, art,
and social life, the name of Anna Jameson shines conspicuously. Notwithstanding the sadness that overshadowed
her earlier days, and other unpropitious
events, by the force of genius she surmounted all opposing difficulties.

Her æsthetic and intellectual pursuits
and studies, combined with her sympa-
thetic nature, ever seeking to ameliorate
the sufferings and privations of others,
have justly won for her a noble name.
She seems to merit the high tribute of
the poet :

"So good a lady, that no tongue could e'er pro-
nounce dishonor of her !"

Her earnest efforts in behalf of the
higher intellectual culture and education of women, and their qualification
for self-support, gave the first impulse
to the great movement for the moral
and social elevation of the sex that has
proved so prolific of beneficent results.*

In glancing back at her early life we
find that she was born at Dublin in 1797.
Mrs. Jameson's father, Brownell Mur-
phy, an associate of Robert Emmett and
Lord Edward Fitzgerald, was happily
saved from sharing their fate by the
cares of a large family.   He had to go
to England to seek a livelihood as a
miniature painter just before the final
catastrophe of Irish patriotism.   After a
fairly successful career at Newcastle, he
removed to London.   Anna, the eldest
of several daughters, was called '' the

---

* We find as the result such institutions established as the
Vassar College, the Wellesley College, and many similar noble
seats of learning, expressly for the intellectual culture of the
fair daughters of our republic, so that in the enlightened
American daughter, wife, and mother, in the free American
home, we may look for the fairest flower and the highest
promise of our advanced civilization.

despot" of the family, but an admired one. Not content with acquiring the French, Italian, and Spanish languages, she also devoted herself to the Oriental disquisitions of Sir William Jones, and composed an Eastern story for the nursery. At sixteen years of age she became a governess to Lord Winchester's family. In the mean time she had fallen in love—or fancied she had—with Captain Robert Jameson. As the result of this, an engagement was contracted between them, and they subsequently were married. The nuptial tie had scarce been formed, however, ere it was rent asunder ; for, three days after, Mr. Jameson announced to her that he intended to spend the day with some of his friends, according to his custom. They being unknown to his wife, he gave her simply the option of going with him or remaining at home. She decided on the latter alternative. Her husband went alone, to dine and spend the evening with his companions, leaving his bride in neglected solitude. Four

years of her married life was a fitting
sequel to such an ominous beginning.
A separation was the inevitable result of
such a union.   Her husband's departure
to the West Indies gave Mrs. Jameson
an opportunity of seeking her own pursuits in literature and art undisturbed ;
but at this juncture she was invited to
accompany her father and Sir Gerard
Noel and his daughter on a pleasant and
luxurious continental tour.

During her travels she kept a diary,
and this was the nucleus of her first
literary production, " The Diary of an
Ennuyée." The book was at once a
success ; so vivid and fresh were some
of its pages, indeed, that one day, when
it fell into the hands of Edward Irving,
he is said to have devoured it eagerly,
and laid it down full of sympathy for
the love-griefs and for the early death
of the poor ennuyée.   A few days later,
at the house of Basil Montague, he was
presented to Anna Jameson, and told
that she was the ennuyée of the
" Diary." His face fell, and turning

to the host, he reproached him for having allowed him to sympathize with the book and its heroine, whom he believed to have been buried in a convent garden.

This ill-assorted marriage seems to have exercised an unfortunate influence over her mind, because it mars in a degree all her works, especially her later ones, by fettering the noblest aspirations of her genius, instinctively feminine, and therefore only capable of feeling the full compass of its powers, when devoted to the true and the good.

In her "Winter Studies and Summer Rambles" she records her observations on Canada and the United States, as far as she travelled. The shadow over these original and spirited pictures is— unhappiness in wedded life ! Everywhere she finds marriage a slavery, a sin, or a sorrow. The shaft in her own bosom she plants in that of every other married pair ; like a person with a painful disease, she hears only of the afflicted, and fancies the world to be a hos-

pital of incurables. She had naturally
a love for the pure and the innocent, a
true woman in her warm sympathies
with her sex ; and had she been fortunate in the connection which possessed
for her, as it does for the noblest and
purest of both sexes, the holiest elements of happiness and the best oppor-
tunities of self-improvement, she would
have been a shining light in the onward
movement of Christian civilization, instead of bowing her woman's soul to
human philosophy and deifying the worship of the beautiful in art.*

Her literary engagements had in-
creased since the temporary separation
from her husband, and she planned and
carried out, among other pursuits, another continental tour, with the view of
visiting the great galleries of art. In
Germany she was greeted with the welcome she deserved as the author of the
" Essay on the Heroines of Shakespeare." Goethe died the year before

* Hale's " Woman's Record."

Mrs. Jameson reached Weimar, but she found there his daughter-in-law, Ottilie von Goethe, and a close intimacy sprang up between the two ladies. During all these months the home in Canada, to which she looked forward whenever her husband should be fairly established in his new position, seemed farther off than ever. She wrote from Germany to her father, with whom her relations were always endearing, that she had " a letter from Canada—as usual very well written, very cold, and very vague ;" but this vagueness gave place at times to words of great bitterness on the part of both. After her return to London and the publication of her " Sketches at Home and Abroad," she was summoned to join her husband at Toronto. On her arrival at New York she was received by the best society, and remained long enough to reproduce her " Characteristics of Women" for American readers. It was during this interval of a few weeks that the writer of this sketch had the privilege of frequently meeting with this gifted and refined lady. The result of her visit to Canada was most unsatisfactory ; for, instead of finding a home of welcome prepared for her, she was coldly met by her husband, and had the further pain of discovering that other and less regular ties had been formed during her absence. Crushed by this neglect and dishonor, she returned to Europe, there to end her days.

In her " Characteristics of Women," traits of character are made palpable by her skilful analysis, which had hitherto escaped the notice of critics. She has classified her heroines into characters of intellect, of passion and imagination, characters of the affections and historical characters. It is not the purpose of the writer, however, to follow, even in outline, the elaborate and interesting analysis which she gives. This is her apostrophe to the characters of passion : " O Love ! thou teacher—O Grief ! thou tamer—O Time ! thou healer of human hearts ! bring hither all your deep and serious revelations. And ye, too, rich fancies of unbruised, unbowed youth ; ye visions of long - cherished hopes ; shadows of unborn joys ; gay colorings of the dawn of existence—whatever memory hath treasured up of bright and beautiful nature or in art ; all soft and delicate images ; all lovely forms ; divinest voices and entrancing melodies ; gleams of sunniest skies and fairer climes—live once more in my heart. Come thronging around me, all inspirations that wait on passion, on power, or beauty.''

In her preface to the American edition of '' Characteristics of Women,'' published in New York, Mrs. Jameson thus wrote : '' My object was not to present a complete commentary on all the female characters of Shakespeare's plays ; such an undertaking would have required much more critical learning than I possess. I must have dived far deeper into that vast, perplexing chaos of tradition, poetry, history, romance, and real life, whence he conjured up spirits of grace, intellect, grandeur, and bade them stand before us clothed in the aspects and passions of humanity. I could not do this, but I selected a few among the creatures of his art for particular consideration, merely to throw into a pleasing and intelligible form some observations on the natural workings of mind and feeling in my own sex, which might lead to good. More than this I never designed ; more than this I never attempted, and what I *have* attempted, I sincerely wish had been done better.''

Her fruitless visit to Toronto ended in October, 1837, and her intercourse with her husband, who allowed her three hundred pounds a year, was thenceforth carried on only by correspondence ; but the letters, which grew less and less frequent, had, like the allowance, ceased altogether before Captain Jameson's death, in 1854. As yet she had been little more than tentative in her work ; its real development was to come. She took, with her adopted niece, Gerardine Bate, a cottage near

London, and applied herself to the
study of Art. In 1840 she says in one of
her letters, " Though there is much to
be done and endured, I cannot say I am
unhappy. I am so engrossed by the interests and sufferings of others I have
no time to think about myself ; besides,
I have just undertaken a new book—a
laborious thing." Mrs. Jameson had
always the happy faculty of pleasing her
readers ; and, consequently, many of
her more elaborate productions to this
day retain their hold upon the cultivat-
ed reader. A contemporary critic has
well said : " It was Mrs. Jameson's task
to lead her readers through the Christian centuries ; to cull for them the early
flowers of Paradise, which Giotto and
Cimabue planted ; to recall the tender-
est forms of medieval fancy, and the
stern thoughts of the men who carried
art as a cross, while they looked for the
speedy consummation of all things in
the second advent of the Lord. She
had, also, to reproduce the mystic beauties of those studios which were cells,

and the dreams of monks who dwelt apart in cloisters." The difficulties of her task were great, but she touched the subjects with a reverent and discreet hand.

Her book, " Sacred and Legendary Art," was received with acclamations at home and abroad. Longfellow wrote : " God bless you for this book ! How very precious it is to me ! Indeed, I can hardly try to express to you the feelings of affection with which I have cherished it from the first moment it reached us. It most amply supplies the cravings of the religious nature." And this enthusiastic praise has elsewhere been echoed in the Old World. Another beautiful work on Christian Art, to which she devoted herself, was the " Life of the Madonna." Nothing can exceed the beauty and finish of this book, with its hundred and sixty-five engravings, and its twenty-seven etchings, illustrating her descriptions in harmonious prose. The last in the series of her great works was " The History of our Lord," which was designed to present the combined results of the piety and industry of nineteen Christian centuries. The pictures were in great numbers, and the themes inexhaustible, for the Christ of history was no passing apparition. While working at this great subject the pen fell from the hand of the gifted and laborious author, and the unfinished manuscript was confided to Lady Eastlake for completion. This noble work closed the long series of the literary labors of Mrs. Jameson. Her entire productions, as recorded in the catalogue of the British Museum, number not less than forty-eight volumes. These works, it is almost superfluous to add, are replete with romantic and historic lore and poetic beauty. The strange mystic symbolism of the early mosaics was to her a legible language ; and in their quaint emblems she could expound the thoughts of the artist of a thousand years ago.

In one of her papers on the great artists, Mrs. Jameson says : " If I were re-

quired to sum up in two great names
whatever the art of painting had contemplated and achieved of highest and
best, I would invoke Raphael and Titian.
The former as the most perfect example
of all that has been accomplished in
the expression of thought through the
medium of form ; the latter of all
that has been accomplished in the expression of life through the medium
of color.   Hence it is, that, while *both*
have given us *mind* and both have given
us *beauty*—Mind, ever the characteristic
of Raphael ; and Beauty, that of Titian !''

Many distinguished families in Rome,
Florence, Dresden, Paris, and elsewhere,
as well as in England, will long remember Mrs. Jameson for her brilliant con-
versational powers, as well as—with the
world of art—for her great service in revealing and inspiring greater love for its
antique treasures.   Indeed, it has been
said that '' not a cypress on Roman hills
exists, or garden on the sweet South
land, a picture or statue in the palaces,

churches, or catacombs, which did not kindle of eager, delightful talk from her.'' She may be said to have lived, notwithstanding her ill-assorted marriage, a busy, brilliant, helpful life, and has left a legacy of high thoughts and incentives to noble aims to all women.

As an illustration of Mrs. Jameson's descriptive power, the following account of her visit to Niagara Falls is present· ed : '' As we prepared to walk to the Crescent Fall, I bound some *crampons* to my feet, like those they use among the Alps, without which I could not have kept my footing on the frozen surface of the snow. As we approached the Table Rock the whole scene assumed a wild and wonderful magnificence ; down came the dark, pure waters, hurrying with them over the edge of the precipice enormous blocks of ice, brought down from Lake Erie. On each side of the falls, from the ledges and overhanging cliffs, were suspended huge icicles, some twenty, some thirty feet in length, thicker than the body of a man, and in

color of a pale green, like the glaciers
of the Alps ; and all the crags below
which projected from the boiling, eddy-
ing waters were incrusted and in a manner built round with ice, which had
formed into immense crystals, like ba-
saltic columns such as I have seen in the
pictures of Staffa and the Giant's Cause-
way ; and every tree and leaf and
branch fringing the rocks and ravines
were wrought in ice. On them and on
the wooden buildings erected near the
Table Rock the spray from the cataract
had accumulated and formed into the
most beautiful crystals and tracery
work ; they looked like houses of glass,
welded and moulded into regular orna-
mental shapes, and hung round with a
rich fringe of icy points. Wherever we
stood we were on unsafe ground, for the
snow, when heaped up, as then, to the
height of three or four feet, frequently
slipped in masses from the bare rock ;
and on its surface the spray, forever
falling, was converted into a sheet of
ice, smooth, compact, and glassy, on

which I could not have stood a moment without my *crampons*.   It was very fearful ; and yet I could not tear myself away, but remained on the Table Rock, even on the very edge of it, till a kind of dreamy fascination came over me. The continuous thunder and might and movement of the lapsing waters held all my vital spirits bound up as by a spell. Then, as at last I turned away, the descending sun broke out, and an iris appeared below the American Falls, one extremity resting on a snow mound ; and motionless, there it hung in the midst of restless terrors, its beautiful but rather pale hues contrasting with the death-like, colorless objects around —it reminded me of the faint, ethereal smile of a dying martyr. . . . It was near midnight when we mounted our sleigh to return to the town of Niagara, and as I remember, I did not utter a word during the whole fourteen miles. The air was still, though keen ; the snow lay around ; the whole earth seemed to slumber in the ghastly, calm repose ; but the heavens were wide awake. There the aurora borealis was holding her revels, and dancing and flashing and varying through all shapes and all hues—pale amber, rose tint, blood red—and the stars shone out with a fitful, restless brilliance ; while every now and then a meteor would shoot athwart the skies or fall to earth ; and all around me was wild and strange and exciting —more like a fever dream than a reality. . . . We drove along the road *above* the falls ; there was the wide river spreading like a vast lake, then narrowing, boiling, and foaming along in a current of eighteen miles an hour, till it swept over the Crescent Rock in a sheet of emerald green, and threw up the silver clouds of spray into the clear blue sky. Now the fresh, luxurious verdure of the woods, relieved against the dark pine forest, added to the beauty of the scene. After dinner I returned to the hotel by the light of a full moon, beneath which the falls looked magnificently mysterious—part glancing silver light, and part dark shadow, mingled with fleecy folds of spray, over which floated a soft, sleepy gleam ; and in the midst of this tremendous velocity of motion and eternity of sound there was a deep, deep repose, as in a dream. It impressed me for the time like something supernatural—a vision, not a reality."

Among her literary friends in this country may be named Irving, Longfellow, Channing, and Catherine Sedgwick ; and when she returned home she was cordially welcomed in London and elsewhere by numerous old friends, among them Mrs. Austin—whose husband Mrs. Jameson refers to as " a hypochondriac"—Fanny Kemble, Rogers, Wordsworth, Mrs. Browning—then Miss Barrett—of whose odd " honeymoon" flitting to Pisa she was some years later the companion ; Marie Edgworth, Lady Byron, Thackeray, etc. On her presentation to the Queen of her " Handbook to the Royal and Private Galleries of the British Nobility," her majesty, with smiling face, thanked Mrs. Jameson, and took it to show Prince Albert.

Her "Commonplace Book of Thoughts, Memories, and Fancies" has justly been characterized as "a beautiful book of a beautiful writer ;" it is replete with words of wisdom, deeply felt and calmly pondered. "Wisdom and the law of kindness" are pre-eminently characteristic of the ethical and critical writings of Mrs. Jameson. "Hers is the commonplace book of no commonplace woman, but of one naturally and habitually meditative." One of her sententious aphorisms, well worth repeating, is the following : "The bread of life is love ; the salt of life is work ; the sweetness of life, poesy ; the water of life, faith."

The following piquant episode we cite from Mrs. Jameson's "Commonplace Book," a volume which has been defined as "full of a thousand melodious suggestions, undertones of sentiment and feeling, and beautiful fragments of thought" : "When travelling in Ire-

land, I stayed over one Sunday in a certain town in the north, and rambled out
early in the morning. It was cold and
wet, the streets empty and quiet, but the
sound of voices drew me in one direc-
tion down a court where there was a
Roman Catholic chapel. It was so
crowded that many of the congregation
stood round the door. I remarked
among them a number of soldiers and
most miserable-looking women. All
made way for me with true national
courtesy, and I entered at the moment
the priest was finishing mass and about
to begin his sermon. There was no pulpit, and he stood on the steps of the
altar—a fine-looking man, with a bright
face, a sonorous voice, and a *very* strong
Irish accent. His text was from Matt.
5 : 43, 44. He began by explaining what
Christ really meant by the words, ' Love
thy neighbor,' then drew a picture in
contrast of hatred and dissension, com-
mencing with dissensions in families, between kindred and between husband and
wife. Then he made a most touching

appeal in behalf of children brought up
in an atmosphere of contention, where
no love is. ' God help them ; God pity
them ! Small chance for them of being
either good or happy, for their young
hearts are saddened and soured with
strife, and they eat their bread in bitterness.' Then he preached patience to
the wives, indulgence to the husbands,
and denounced scolds and quarrelsome
women in a manner that seemed to
glance at recent events. ' When ye are
found in the streets vilifying and slan-
dering one another—ay, fighting and
tearing each other's hair—do ye think
ye're women ? No, ye're not ; ye're devils incarnate, and ye'll go where the devils
will be fit companions for ye ! ' (Here
some women near me, with long black
hair streaming down, fell on their knees,
sobbing with contrition.) He then went
on in the same strain of homely eloquence to the evils of political and religious hatred, and quoted the text, ' If
it be possible, as much as lieth in you,
live peaceably with all men.' ' I'm a

Catholic,' he went on, 'and I believe in the truth of my own religion above all others. I'm convinced, by long study and observation, it's the best that is ; but what then ? Do you think I hate my neighbor because he thinks differently ? Do ye think I *mane* to force my religion down other people's throats ? ' . . . The fights, domestic and political, the rich without care for the poor, and the poor without food or work—all arose from nothing but the want of love. ' Down on your knees,' he exclaimed, ' and ask God's mercy and pardon ; and as ye hope to find it, ask pardon of one another for every angry word ye have spoken, for every uncharitable thought that has come into your minds ; and if any man or woman have aught against his neighbor, no matter what, let it be plucked out of his heart before he leaves this place ; let it be forgotten at the door of this chapel. Let me, your pastor, have no more *rason* to be ashamed of you, as if I were set over wild *bastes* instead of Christian men and women ! '

After more in this fervid strain, which I cannot recollect, he gave his blessing in the same earnest, heart-felt manner. I never saw a congregation more attentive, more reverent, and apparently more touched and edified." . . . A very different sketch is the following from her versatile pen ; but it will doubtless interest many readers. She writes from Brighton, and thus refers to the eminent clergyman of that day, Rev. Mr. Robertson : " My great pleasure is to hear Mr. Robertson preach. I never heard anything to equal him in *eloquence*— really fine speaking, not mere fervor and fluency ; a logical distribution of his subject and an entire command of himself and his own power, as well as of his audience."

As the following letter possesses a compound interest, it may be well to transcribe it in full. It was Mr. Longfellow who thus addressed her from Cambridge, Mass. :

" DEAR MRS. JAMESON : Having many

friends, who are your friends and ad-
mirers, and none more so than my own
wife, I venture to smuggle myself in
among them at this season, and wish you
all the good wishes of the New Year. I
beg you to accept a volume of poems
which I have just published, and in
which I hope there may be something
that will give you pleasure—you, who
have given me so much, particularly
your last work, 'Sacred and Legendary
Art.' How very precious it is to me;
indeed, I shall hardly try to express to
you the feelings of affection with which
I have cherished it from the first moment
it reached us. It most amply supplies
the cravings of the religious sentiment,
of the spiritual nature within. It pro-
duces in my soul the same effect that
great organists have produced by lay-
ing slight weights upon certain keys of
their instruments, thus keeping an un-
broken flow of melody, while their fin-
gers are busy with the other keys and
stops. And there let these volumes lie,
pressing just enough upon my thoughts

to make perpetual music. God bless
you for this book !
        " Your sincere friend,
            " HENRY W. LONGFELLOW."

It may not be thought inappropriate,
indeed, here to cite the opinion of a
critic in the *Irish Quarterly Review*, who
thus wrote : " There is not one in the
whole noble band of English female
writers from the Duchess of Newcastle,
of whose life of her husband Charles
Lamb wrote, ' No casket is rich enough,
no casing sufficiently durable to honor
and keep safe such a jewel '—to Hannah
More, of whom Sydney Smith said, *ban-
tering*, that he spoke timidly of her, as
of a mysterious and superior being—
more worthy of the great praise bestowed upon her works than Mrs. Jameson." The same authority continues :
" Growing up in all the refined natural
tastes of a very woman, Mrs. Jameson
has become the mental anatomist of her
sex. It must be acknowledged that,
while claiming the fullest and highest

position in the ranks of human nature, she has never. become in the most remote degree a woman's rights advocate. With ability of the highest order, gifted with energy of mind, and endowed with great and eloquent powers of expression, she has always been mindful of the truth, that the qualities making woman glorious and equal to man are not the qualities which induce women to demand equality with men."

Her essays on the social relations of mothers and governesses—a topic which she was well qualified to discuss, from her own varied experience—are marked by wise suggestions, and many of them have been applied to the removal of then existing evils. In her later years she took up a succession of subjects, all bearing on the same principles of active benevolence, and the best way of carrying them into operation. Indeed, it has been remarked that during the later part of her life Mrs. Jameson was considered not only the patron, but the counsellor, of her sex in England.

Women in mental anguish needing con-
solation and advice " fled to her, as to
a convent, for protection and guid-
ance." Her published appeals and
efforts in behalf of her dependent sis-
terhood naturally led them to seek her
assistance, sympathy, and counsel ; and
she devoted herself generously to minis-
tering to their succor and aid.

A glimpse of the personal struggles
through which she passed may be
caught in the following extract from
one of her letters : " Outwardly I stand
in the world an enviable being ; inward-
ly it is a hard struggle. Of how many
women might the history be comprised
in these few words, ' She lived, suffered,
and was buried ! ' " Yet at the time
she wrote to another : " I accept about
one invitation out of three, for I have
something better to do than to stand
dangling in a court circle talking nothing." She seems to have devoted herself to literature and art not only from
a pure love of such studies, but because
it was necessary to her support and

those of her family who were dependent upon her.

From her earliest recollections she seems to have had an instinctive love of natural beauty ; and this sense of the beautiful in nature gave her the zest for poetry. Shakespeare's dramas she had read when only ten years old ; the " Tempest" and " Cymbeline" were the plays she liked and knew the best. Nor should it be forgotten, as characteristic of the quality of her child life, her sensibility to music.

Those who knew her best attest by their glowing tribute to her memory how much she was loved and honored in the domestic circles that she visited, both in her native land and elsewhere.

Her death, in March, 1860, which was sudden, was caused by inflammation of the lungs, superinduced by cold caught during a winter visit from Brighton to the British Museum. There is a touching incident connected with the " Memoirs of Anna Jameson." While this tribute of loving remembrance was

being prepared for the press, her niece
died, and it was left to Mrs. Oliphant
to bestow the final revision as a tribute
of love to both.   So that this very graceful sketch of a very graceful writer has
an additional element of pathos in the
fact that the volume is an epitaph at
once on its heroine and its author.

In fine, no one can read the loving
biography of Mrs. Jameson, by her
favorite niece, in connection with the
few pages of the postscript, without a
pang of sympathy and pity.   "There we
find how hard was the last chapter of
Geraldine's existence, after many years
of not unprosperous nor unhappy, yet
far from tranquil married life, which followed her union with Robert Macpher-
son, once a very well-known figure in
Rome.   He died in 1873, leaving her
penniless and overwhelmed with debt.
It may well be said that the writer of the
book has given us with the subject of
her biography her own touching memorial.

Analyzing for us the great art produc-

tions of the ages, Mrs. Jameson's name
is also associated with a series of beneficent services in behalf of her sex. In
the opinion and words of Lady Eastlake,
' the most valuable of all.' She began
her literary career by analyzing books,
she proceeded to analyze works of art,
and she ended by analyzing society. It
was a natural supplement to a course of
varied personal experience, and no little
struggle, that her attention should be
directed to the great moral questions of
the day, and especially to those affect-
ing the education, occupations, and
maintenance of her own sex. Her early
essay on the ' Relative Social Position
of Mothers and Governesses ' is a masterpiece. She knew both sides ; and in
no respect does she more clearly prove
the falseness of the position she de-
scribes than in the certainty with which
she predicts its eventual reform. . . .
In her later years she took up a succession of subjects all bearing on the same
principles of active benevolence, and the
best ways of carrying them into prac-

tice.   Sisters of charity, hospitals, peni-
tentiaries, prisons, and workhouses all
claimed her interest ; all more or less
included under those definitions of ' the
communion of love and communion of
labor,' which are inseparably connected
with her memory.   To the clear and
temperate forms in which she brought
the results of her convictions before her
friends in the form of private lectures,
subsequently printed, may be traced the
source whence living reformers and
philanthropists took counsel and courage.''

WASHINGTON IRVING.

Born 1783, died 1859.

" One kindly advised him to avoid the ludicrous ; another to shun the pathetic ; a third assured him that he was tolerable at description, but cautioned him to leave narrative alone ; while a fourth declared that he had a very pretty knack at turning a story, and was really entertaining when in a pensive mood, but was grievously mistaken if he imagined himself to possess a spirit of humor."— *Irving's account of himself in his " Sketch Book."*

WASHINGTON IRVING.

IN a sequestered rural retreat, some twenty-five miles from the din of city life, half hid among thick foliage, through which the tourist may catch glimpses of an antique, grotesque-looking cottage known as " Sunnyside," was the home of Washington Irving. It is an enchanting little nook, charmingly diversified with upland, lawn, and dell, rock and rivulet, with no sound to disturb save that of rustling leaf, humming insect, or voice of feathered songster. There is an air of quaintness about it even yet ; for it was, to some extent, an exponent of the mind and taste of its illustrious occupant. This picturesque domicile he had modernized and decorated with sundry improvements ; and as nature had already decked it with leafy luxuriance and beauty, we need not wonder that these environments charmed Irving's fancy and taste, or that it should have become the site of attraction to his legend-loving pen ; and thus it has become charmed with a spirit of fairy legend and romance that will hereafter ever hover over the spot.

Let the pen that has so felicitously chronicled the legendary lore of the Hudson be here cited for further details :

'' It was a lowly edifice, built in the time of the Dutch dynasty, and stood on a green bank, overshadowed by trees, from which it peeped forth upon the Great Tappan Zee, so famous among early Dutch navigators. Though but of small dimensions, yet, like many small people, it is of mighty spirit, and values itself greatly on its antiquity, being one of the oldest edifices for its size in the whole country. This doughty and valorous little pile claims to be an ancient seat of empire—I may rather say, an empire in itself—and, like all em-

pires, great and small, has had its grand
historical epochs. Its origin, in truth,
dates far back in that remote region
commonly called the fabulous age, in
which vulgar fact becomes mystified
and tinted up with delectable fiction.
A bright, pure spring welled up at the
foot of the green bank ; a wild brook
came babbling down a neighboring
ravine, and threw itself into a little
woody cove in front of the mansion. It
was indeed as quiet and sheltered a
nook as the heart of man could require
in which to take refuge from the cares
and troubles of the world ; and as such
it had been chosen in old times, by Wolfert Acker, one of the privy councillors
of the renowned Peter Stuyvesant.
This worthy but ill-starred man had led
a weary and worried life throughout the
stormy reign of the chivalric Peter,
being one of those unlucky wights with
whom the world is ever at variance, and
who are kept in a continual fume and
fret by the wickedness of mankind. At
the time of the subjugation of the prov-

ince by the English, he retired hither in high dudgeon, with the bitter determination to bury himself from the world, and live here in peace and quietness for the remainder of his days.

" In token of this fixed resolution he inscribed over his door the favorite Dutch motto, ' Lust in Rust ' (pleasure in repose). The mansion was thence called ' Wolfert's Rust ' — Wolfert's Rest ; but in process of time the name was vitiated into Wolfert's Roost, probably from its quaint cockloft look, or from its having a weather-cock perched on every gable.

" Here, then, have I set up my rest, surrounded by the recollections of early days and the mementoes of the historian of the Manhattoes, with that glorious river before me which flows with such majesty through his works, and which has ever been to me a river of delight. I thank God I was born on the banks of the Hudson. I think it an invaluable advantage to be born and brought up in the neighborhood of some grand and

noble object in nature—a river, a lake,
or a mountain. We make a friendship
with it, we in a manner ally ourselves to
it for life. It remains an object of our
pride and affection, a rallying-point to
call us home again after all our wanderings. 'The things which we have
learned in our childhood,' says an old
writer, 'grow up with our soul and
unite themselves to it.' So it is with
the scenes among which we have passed
our early days ; they influence the whole
course of our thoughts and feelings, and
I fancy I can trace much of what is good
and pleasant in my own heterogeneous
compound to my early companionship
with this glorious river. In the warmth
of my youthful enthusiasm I used to
clothe it with moral attributes and almost to give it a soul. I admired its
frank, bold, honest character, its noble
sincerity and perfect truth. Here was
no specious, smiling, surface covering
the dangerous sand-bar or perfidious
rock, but a stream deep as it was broad,
and bearing with honorable faith the

bark that trusted to its waves. I gloried
in its simple, quiet, majestic, epic flow,
ever straight forward. Once, indeed,
it turns aside for a moment, forced from
its course by opposing mountains, but
it struggles bravely through them and
immediately resumes its straightforward
march. Behold, thought I, an emblem
of a good man's course through life,
ever simple, open, and direct ; or if,
overpowered by adverse circumstances,
he deviate into error, it is but momen-
tary, he soon recovers his onward and
honorable career, and continues it to
the end of his pilgrimage. The Hudson
is, in a manner, my first and last love,
and after all my wanderings and seeming infidelities I return to it with a heart-
felt preference over all the other rivers
in the world.''

Among the clustered beauties and historic relics of '' Sunnyside'' may be
mentioned the rich trailing ivy which
almost covers the study window. This
was planted from a slip originally
brought from Melrose Abbey and pre-

sented by Sir Walter Scott to Mrs. Fen-
wick, a friend of Irving's, and who was
celebrated in song by Burns. Here
lived our first, if not foremost, representative in American letters ; and here
he spent the last twenty happy years of
his honored and fruitful life. It is not
surprising that one to whom American
letters owes so much should also, by
his distinguished literary fame, as well
as his eminent personal character, have
won from so many loving testimonials
of personal esteem. As the writer of
the present sketch had the good fortune
to share the honor of his acquaintance
for over a score of years, he may be permitted to add this to those numerous
'tributes to the memory of the genial and
gifted author of the " Sketch Book,'"
" Geoffrey Crayon, Gent."

When Mr. Irving was in England, and
before he commenced his literary career,.
his friends proposed that he should be
introduced to Mr. William Roscoe, of
Liverpool, the historian, of Leo X. and
other well-known works. Acting upon

the suggestion, he visited Mr. Roscoe. Unknown to Mr. Irving, some friend had, previously to their interview, put into the hands of Mr. Roscoe several of the early contributions of Mr. Irving which were printed in the " Portfolio." Among them was a paper on the " Aborigines of America," and it was to this that Mr. Roscoe referred with especial commendation. Mr. Irving, in a quiet way, replied that he fully agreed with him in his estimate of *that* paper, as it was the production of a friend of his, Mr. Henry Brevoort, of New York. From that time Roscoe became interested in Irving's career ; and the reader will not need to be reminded of the fact, as it is on record in the " Sketch Book." This incident suggests another and later event, which may not be inaptly cited here.

The description of the meeting of Irving and Scott is so characteristic of both those eminent men that it cannot fail to be of lasting interest. Late in the evening of August 29th, 1817, Irving reached the town of Selkirk, where he lodged for the night. " I had come from Edinburgh," he wrote, " partly to visit Melrose Abbey and its vicinity, but chiefly to get a sight of the ' mighty minstrel of the north.' I had a letter of introduction to him from Thomas Campbell, the poet, and had reason to think, from the interest he had taken in some of my earlier scribblings, that a visit from me would not be deemed an intrusion. On the following morning I set off in a post-chaise for the abbey. On the way thither I stopped at the gate of Abbotsford, and sent the postilion to the house with the letter of introduction and my card, on which I had written that I was on my way to the ruins of Melrose Abbey, and wished to know whether it would be agreeable to him to receive a visit from me in the course of the morning. The noise of the vehicle had disturbed the quiet of the establishment. Out sallied the warder of the castle—a black greyhound—and leaping on one of the blocks of stone, began a furious barking ; his alarm brought out the whole garrison of dogs, 'both puppy, mongrel, whelp and hound, and curs of low degree,' all open-mouthed and vociferous. In a little while the 'lord of the castle' himself made his appearance. I knew him at once, by the descriptions I had read and heard and the likenesses I had seen of him. He was tall and of a large and powerful frame ; his dress was simple, almost rustic—an old green shooting-coat, with a dog-whistle at the buttonhole ; brown linen pantaloons, stout shoes that tied at the ankles, and a white hat that had evidently seen service. He came limping up the gravel walk, aiding himself by a stout walking staff, but moving rapidly and with vigor. By his side jogged along a large iron-gray stag-hound of the most grave deportment, taking no part in the clamor of the canine rabble, but seeming to consider himself bound, for the dignity of the house, to give me a courteous reception. Before Scott had reached the gate he called out in a

hearty tone, welcoming me to Abbotsford.

" I soon felt myself quite at home and
my heart in a glow with the cordial welcome I experienced. I had thought to
make a mere morning visit, but found I
was not to be let off so lightly. 'You
must not think our neighborhood is to
be read in a morning, like a newspaper,'
said Scott. 'It takes several days of
study for an observant traveller that has
a relish for auld-world trumpery. After
breakfast you shall make your visit to
Melrose Abbey. I shall not be able to
accompany you, as I have some household affairs to attend to ; but I will put
you in charge of my son Charles, who is
very learned in all things touching the
old ruin and the neighborhood it stands
in ; and he and my friend, Johnny
Bower, will tell you the whole truth
about it, with a great deal more that
you are not called upon to believe un-
less you be a true and nothing-doubting
antiquary. To-morrow we will take a
look at the Yarrow, and the next day we

will drive over to Dryburgh Abbey,
which is a fine old ruin well worth your
seeing'—in a word, before Scott had got
through with his plan, I found myself
committed for a visit of several days ;
and it seemed as if a little realm of romance had opened suddenly before
me. . . . On the following morning
the sun darted his beams from over the
hills through the low lattice window.   I
rose at an early hour and looked out between the branches of eglantine which
overhung the casement.   To my surprise, Scott was already up and forth,
seated on a fragment of stone chatting
with the workmen employed on the new
building.   I soon joined, when he talked
about his proposed plans of Abbotsford.
Happy would it have been for him could
he have contented himself with his delightful little vine-covered cottage and
the simple yet hearty, hospitable style
in which he lived at the time of my
visit.   The great pile of Abbotsford,
with the huge expense it entailed upon
him—of servants, retainers, guests, and

baronial style, was a drain upon his purse, a tax upon his exertions, and a weight upon his mind that finally crushed him. . . . During several days that I had passed there Scott was in admirable vein ; from early morn until dinner-time he was rambling about with me ; no time was reserved for himself ; he seemed as if his only occupation was to entertain me, and yet I was almost an entire stranger to him—one of whom he knew nothing but an idle book I had written, and which some years before had amused him. But such was Scott. The conversation of my host was frank, hearty, picturesque, and dramatic. At the time of my visit he inclined to the comic rather than the grave in his anecdotes and stories ; he relished a joke or a trait of humor in social intercourse, and laughed with right good will. It was delightful to observe the generous spirit in which he spoke of all his literary contemporaries. . . . In fine, I consider it one of the greatest advantages that I have derived from my literary career that it has elevated me into genial communion with such a spirit.''

To complete the touching picture— the greeting and the parting of two kindred immortals—Irving's own description of their last interview is annexed :

'' I was in London when Scott arrived after his attack' of paralysis, on his way to the continent in search of health.   I received a note from Lockhart begging me to come and take dinner with Scott and himself the next day.   When I entered the room Scott grasped my hand and looked me steadfastly in the face. ' Time has dealt gently with you, my friend, since we parted,' he exclaimed— he referred to the difference in himself since we had met.   At dinner I could see that Scott's mind was failing ; he was painfully conscious of it himself. He would talk with much animation, and we would listen with the most respectful attention ; but there was an effort and an embarrassment in his manner—he knew all was not right.   It was very distressing, and we tried to keep up the conversation between ourselves, that Sir Walter might talk as little as possible. After dinner he took my arm to walk upstairs, which he did with difficulty. He turned and looked in my face and said, ' They need not tell a man his mind is not affected when his body is as much affected as mine.' . . . This was my last interview with Scott." Few could have valued his friend more highly or deplored his loss more keenly than did Irving his early and fast friend, Scott. These are some of his words : " Of his public character and merits all the world can judge. His works have incorporated themselves with the thoughts and concerns of the whole civilized world for a quarter of a century, and have had a controlling influence over the age in which he lived. But when did a human being ever exercise an influence more salutary and benignant ? Who is there that, on looking back over a great portion of his life, does not find the genius of Scott administering to his pleasures, beguiling his cares, soothing his lonely sorrows? When I consider how much he has thus contributed to the better hours of my past existence, I bless my stars that cast my lot in his days; and as a tribute of gratitude for his friendship and veneration for his memory, I cast this humble stone upon his cairn.''

The writer of this paper first knew Mr. Irving in the year 1837, through an introductory letter from Mr. Charles Macfarlane, the author of several well-known books on Italy, Turkey, etc., who met Mr. Irving at Milan and elsewhere during their continental travels. It is with a feeling of unmingled satisfaction and pleasure that he looks back to those early days, as Mr. Irving uniformly evinced a warm interest and sympathy in co-operating by his influence and name in an enterprise which involved the whole '' republic of letters.'' A few years later, upon the occasion of a banquet given in New York in honor of Mr. Charles Dickens' first visit to this country, Mr. Irving was requested to preside. Although against his inclination, being unaccustomed to make public addresses, yet his modesty was overruled, and, under protest, he had to become chairman. He predicted his failure, and the event verified it ; for after a few introductory words he paused, and then made an effort to address the great assembly ; but again becoming embarrassed, took refuge in the announcement of the toast, " Charles Dickens, the guest of the nation." The scene was one the writer will not forget. Resuming his seat amid the responsive and tumultuous applause, Irving whispered to those near to him, " There, I told you I should fail, and I have done it." This amusing incident suggests another, which was almost the counterpart of the above.

In 1842, when in London, Mr. Irving was an invited guest at the meeting of the " Literary Fund" dinner, which was presided over by Prince Albert. The company was a brilliant constellation of intellectual luminaries—historians, scientists, and poets ; among them were Hallam, Talford, Moore, Campbell, James, Lord Mahon, and Edward Everett, our minister.   Irving was, of course, toasted ; and it is said that his responsive speech was compressed within the narrow limits of *nine words !*

Passing over a rather extended interval, during which occurred Mr. Irving's absence abroad, the next incident memory recalls is that of the public welcome which was tendered to Irving by the publishers and booksellers of the city of New York upon his return to his native land.   This was in the autumn of 1855. The fame of our author was then at its zenith, and many of our most distinguished men of letters assembled to do him honor.   Among them were James Fenimore Cooper, Daniel Webster, George Bancroft, and many others.   Mr. Irving on this occasion, being among his literary confrères and his good friends the publishers, felt more at his ease, and he consequently got through with his after-dinner speech without embarrassment.

Mr. Irving, who was a friend and frequent visitor of Mr. Astor, doubtless encouraged, conjointly with Dr. J. G. Cogswell, the project of founding a public Library, when Mr. Astor, desiring to render a public benefit to the city of New York, was still undecided what form it should take. Whether a Library was first suggested by them, or whether it was due entirely to the impulse of his own generous purpose, it may safely be affirmed that such a project could not fail of meeting with the hearty concurrence of his friends. The grand result, in the establishment of the library, is a lasting matter of gratulation to all lovers of learning and progressive civilization ; while it will ever shed lustre alike upon its munificent founder, its illustrious president, and its accomplished superintendent.

At one of the writer's visits to Mr. Irving at Sunnyside he found the author

in his *sanctum* surrounded with his manu-
scripts and books, with pen in hand ; he
rose to greet his unexpected visitor with
his uniform courtesy and cordiality.
Passing from his study to the parlor, he
was introduced to some ladies—Mr. Irving's nieces, whom he styled his guar-
dian angels—adding he " supposed that
few old bachelors were so fortunate as
himself—they were so careful of him."
In the spring of 1859, in response to Mr.
Irving's kind invitation to meet some of
his literary friends, the writer well remembers the unmingled pleasure of that
delightful visit, so unalloyed was the
enjoyment alike of host and guests. But
little did that joyous company imagine
what a sad reverse was so soon to over-
shadow us, that to most of us it was to
prove our last interview with Irving. It
was the common remark of his guests
that Mr. Irving seemed in unusually
good spirits and so exuberant of genial
humor, so full of reminiscences of his
European travels, and personal anecdotes of his literary friends abroad. Be-

fore assembling for dinner Mr. Irving escorted us about his beautiful grounds, which his gardener had skilfully laid out so as to combine the picturesque effects of meadow, lawn, ravine, and rivulet, garnished with flowers and festooned with luxuriant foliage.

At the table the social intercourse was most cordial, for all seemed to have caught inspiration from the happy host, who kept up an animated narrative of his travels and adventures abroad and the wonders of the Old World. To attempt to reproduce them in detail would, however, be doing serious injustice alike to their author and the reader. One or two items must suffice. When in Paris Irving became acquainted with Vanderlyn, who painted the " Landing of Columbus" which now hangs in the rotunda of the Capitol at Washington. In Madrid, he said, he enjoyed special privileges, being allowed apartments in the palace of the Alhambra ; and while there he produced some of his choicest works—" The Alhambra," " Conquest

of Granada," and "Life and Voyages
of Columbus."

The last-named work made its appearance in 1828, from the press of John
Murray, his London publisher, who
paid for the manuscript three thousand
guineas. Mr. Irving referred to his
many pleasurable interviews at Murray's
house in Albemarle Street, where most
of the leading literary notabilities were
accustomed to gather as at a literary
club. Here he met Moore, Campbell,
Byron, Rogers, Sydney Smith, Scott,
and Lockhart. After we had retired from
the dining-room, Mr. Irving did the
writer the honor to escort him over his
lawn, after which we sat on a rustic bench
which overlooked the Hudson. Here he
again spoke of his old love of the nooks
and corners of old London, and the antiquities of England's cathedral towns, its
rural retreats, its moss-crowned castles
and historic sites. His allusion to the
continental antiquities, and especially to
the legendary Rhine, seemed to fire him
with something of the fervor of a first

love. When the writer referred to his having read the "Sketch Book" long before he had the pleasure of knowing its author, he responded that, after his "Knickerbocker," the "Sketch Book," with its unexpected success, was followed by "Bracebridge Hall" and "The Traveller" with comparative facility ; but that his "Life of Columbus" cost him more hard labor than any other of his productions. We visited his cosey little library—a *bijou* of a study—walled round with pictures, including Jarvis's portrait and bust of himself, busts of Dante, Rogers, and books, including many choice gifts from literary friends. In the rear was a lounge screened by a curtain, upon which our author would indulge an occasional *siesta* or beguile himself with some pleasing reverie. In the drawing-room were also indications of the refined taste of its occupants ; many objects of *virtu* and curiosities brought from remote places were to be seen, as well as paintings by Leslie,

Stuart Newton, and some original sketches by Cruikshank.

It is not difficult to infer the source of his many-hued characters and the odd situations in which he places some of them ; his sketches doubtless are the result of his early habits of close observation, as well as fondness for adventure and travel. He said, indeed, that he was always fond of visiting strange characters and scenes, and it has been his fortune to have had his roving passion gratified.

The legendary lore of the Rhine and the Hartz Mountains proved so potent a charm to the lover of the marvellous, that he resolved to attempt a series of sketches somewhat upon the same model, touching the woods and streams of America. With what singular success this projected resolution was achieved it is needless to speak. If the castellated peaks of Germany, so celebrated in romance and song, have become the attraction of the Old World, it would seem to require no prophetic spirit to predict the results of a similar kind from the magic and ideal pen of our author for the New World. His weird fancy, which has thrown such an imperishable charm over Sleepy Hollow, decked the banks of the Hudson with poetic associations, and crowned the hoary fastnesses of the Catskills with a species of Dutch mythology, has assuredly invested with the witchery of ideal beauty some of the great natural glories of America.

In the picturesque words of a scholarly writer of our day : * "The shore at Tarrytown, stretching backward to Sleepy Hollow, the broad waters of the Tappan Zee, the airy heights of the summer Catskills, were suffused with the rosy light of literature by the kindly genius of Washington Irving. Burns and Scott have made every hill, and stream, and bird, and flower of their beloved land reflected individually and fondly in Scottish tale and song. The

---

* Dr. J. M. Taylor.

Scotchman, with his deep and strong national sentiment, murmurs wherever he goes the legendary music of the Ayr and the Doon, of the laverock and the mavis, the Scottish landscape and the Scottish legend. Irving's genius was what, in the old English phrase, would have been called sauntering ; it cast the glamour of idlesse over our sharp, positive, and busy American life. Rip Van Winkle, the indolent and kindly vagabond, asserts the charm of daydream and loitering against all the engrossing hurry of lucrative activity. At first he and the grotesque Knickerbocker heroes were solitary figures in our letters ; and still Rip Van Winkle lounges idly by, and the vagabond of the Hudson is an unwasting figure of the imagination, the earliest, constant, gentlest satirist of American life."

When Wilkie, the painter, and Irving, the writer, were rambling about Europe *ad libitum*, they at length turned their steps toward that land of old romance and chivalry—Spain—where they were struck with the resemblances of many scenes and incidents to passages found in "The Arabian Nights." This suggested to the artist, who urged our author to write some sketches and historiettes in the vein of that old fascination ; and as a result we have that charming work " Tales of the Alhambra." No writer of note, we believe, was more controlled by impulse or moods of mind in doing the best literary work than was Washington Irving ; indeed, he confessed his inability to do justice to himself or his subject except when so inclined or when the poetic afflatus was upon him. When once got to work, however, he hardly gave himself time for rest or refreshment, so anxious was he to keep at work while he felt the impulse to do so. When at Madrid, he confessed that " he never found outside the walls of his study any enjoyment equal to that of being at his writing desk, and also that some of the happiest hours of his life were those passed in the composition of his books." When ad-

vised to employ an amanuensis, he said
that he " could not get along with that
process ; brain and pen, with him, must
be harnessed together ; and that his inspiration spells were capricious and not
to be controlled."

When in London, on a certain occasion Moore called upon Irving, and finding him engaged in writing, and not
wishing to interrupt him, left him undisturbed and unconscious of the visit.

There is such a remarkable difference
between Irving's " Knickerbocker" and
his " Sketch Book"—so much of pathos
and fine sentiment in the one and so
much of sarcasm and satire in the other
—that we scarcely recognize the identity
of authorship. Scott's high compliment
to the first-named production is worth
quoting ; it reads as follows :

" I beg you to accept my best thanks
for the uncommon degree of entertain·
ment which I have received from the
most excellently jocose history of New
York. I am sensible that, as a stranger
to American parties and politics, I must

lose much of the concealed satire of the piece ; but I must own that, looking at the simple and obvious meaning only, I have never read anything so closely resembling the style of Dean Swift as the annals of Diedrich Knickerbocker.''

When the writer first read the '' Sketch Book'' in London he little expected to have the pleasure of knowing personally its distinguished author ; few books of that early day made so pleasurable and abiding an impression ; and among its choicest chapters, that descriptive of Westminster Abbey was the chief. Scarcely less delightful are his sketches of old-time rural life and scenery ; for example, the following : '' It is a pleasing sight of a Sunday morning, when the bell is sending its sober melody across the quiet fields, to behold the peasantry, in their best finery, with ruddy faces and modest cheerfulness, thronging tranquilly along the green lanes to church.'' And at evening, '' about their cottage doors, apparently exulting in the humble comforts which their own hands have spread around them."

His descriptions of memorable persons and places in the British metropolis are no less felicitous and artistic. While it may seem quite superfluous at the present time to refer to the characteristic claims of a work that has already become a classic of our literature, yet it is interesting to refer to Irving's own confession, which may be accepted as a clue to the rare charm of his style. He says that he "longed to tread in the footsteps of antiquity, to loiter about the ruined castle, to meditate on the moss-grown tower—to escape, in short, from the commonplace realities of the present, and to lose himself among the shadowy grandeur of the past." His "Sketch Book" thus originated while he and his brother Peter were walking over Westminster bridge one dull, foggy day, when Washington began reciting some of the old Dutch stories which he had heard at Tarrytown in his early days. The thought of writing them occurred to him, and he suddenly exclaimed : " I have it ! I'll go home and make memoranda of these for a book." This he did on the following day—one of the darkest and dullest of London fogs— and then wrote out, by the light of a candle, his " Legend of Sleepy Hollow."

There is an incident connected with Irving's " Sketch Book" which it may be worth while to refer to. When visiting Shakespeare's house at Stratford, and lingering as he did there, he called at the Red Horse Inn for refreshments and lodging. Here he was accustomed to sit up late at nights writing for his " Sketch Book,"* and he occasionally

---

* After his return from his official mission to the Spanish court, Mr. Irving made frequent visits to the Astor Library, in consultation of authorities, for completion of his " Life of Washington," as well as when attending the stated meetings of the Board of Trustees. The writer well remembers his last visit, which was in the early autumn of 1859, when he came to inspect the library extension by the erection of the second hall. On this occasion he did not seem to be in his usual health and vigor, yet he did not manifest any premonitory signs of an approaching crisis or the sad event which was so soon to follow. In a cheerful conversation with his friend, Dr. Cogswell, he remarked : " What might have been my destiny could I have commanded these treasures

took the liberty of stirring up the fire with the steel poker that he found there, much to the annoyance of the old landlady, who was unaccustomed to having such a late visitor. Afterward, however, when she discovered that she was mentioned in that book, she had the poker dignified with the title of " Geoffrey Crayon's sceptre." Visitors to the shrine of the great dramatist doubtless

---

in my youth !" These significant words were the last he uttered as he took a rapid survey of the library. About two months later came the sad calamity to us of his demise at Sunnyside. The mournful intelligence soon cast a gloom over the hearts of all lovers of his refined and genial productions, at home and abroad ; and every demonstration of sorrow was indicated by the community at large. The trustees of the library recorded their profound sense of esteem, using, among other words, the following : " We deplore the loss which the Astor Library has sustained in the death of Washington Irving, its first President, the chosen friend of the founder of the library, and first named by him in the original act of donation as a trustee—a selection fully justified by the admirable qualities of Mr. Irving."

On Sunday, November 27th, 1859, Mr. Irving for the last time attended Divine service, at Christ Church, Tarrytown, of which he was a member and warden. On the following day he took his accustomed walk in the adjacent meadows, and in the evening he sat watching from his parlor window the beautiful autumnal sunset—so symbolic and so prophetic of his own life—declining in the golden west.

have heard the story and handled the sceptre.

When the story of " Rip Van Winkle" was written, the author was living at Kinderhook, on the Hudson, some distance from the *locale* of the legend ; and as he had not visited the mountain range prior to its publication, it is not a little remarkable that the details of the scene should have proved topographically so accurate.

Some time after its publication, Mr. Irving was on a visit there for the first time, and, as is usual, the guide pointed out to him the scene of the redoubtable and drowsy Dutchman. He also led him to the turn in the road, at the entrance to a deep ravine, to Rip Van Winkle's house, over the entrance to which is an enormous sign representing Rip as he awoke from his long " nap" in the Catskills. He listened to the rehearsal of his own legend with exemplary patience, pleased to find his *imaginary* description of its locality so singularly verified by fact. He quietly retired without revealing himself as the author.

On a certain occasion Irving was returning home from New York, and found himself in the cars next to an Irish woman with two noisy children that she could not keep quiet. Mr. Irving took one of them in his arms, caressed it, and when the woman got out of the car she thanked him, saying, "You must be a kind, good father, sir." "No," replied our author, "I am, unfortunately, an old bachelor." The children showed their love for him at the Tarrytown church by often garnishing Irving's pew.

His kindly nature is seen in an incident that occurred once in his orchard. He caught a young lad up in one of his apple trees; instead of sending him away with rebuke, he simply called up to him, saying, "If you like apples, there is yonder a fine rosy one, and I will help you to get it."

The asthma was beginning to affect his health when he had just completed

the "Life of Washington;" in addition
to this latent disease he suffered occasionally from chills and fever, contracted
when on a tour westward. Insomnia
was the last form of interruption to his
previous uniform health. In conse-
quence of his inability of obtaining sufficient sleep he became subject to frequent fits of despondency.

On retiring, he said : "I must ar-
range my pillows for another weary
night ;" and some indistinct utterances
about the "end" were the last words
from his lips ; for, with a slight cry as
of pain, he fell in the presence of his attendant, and when the physician arrived
life was extinct. His sun had set, and
not with less glory than marked the
sunset he had witnessed. Shortly before he passed from our horizon of vision his own prophetic words were, "I
am getting ready to go ; shutting up
doors and windows ;" and in response
to the inquiry of his niece one morning,
after a sleepless night, he said, "I am
apt to be rather fatigued, my dear, with

my night's rest." Humor and pathos,
the characteristics of his writings, were
his personal characteristics to the last.
So passed away from us the gifted and
kindly Washington Irving. His fruitful
and picturesque life, which, as we measure uniformly by years, reached just beyond the "threescore and ten;" but
how much have those laborious years
enriched our literary wealth ! Not only
has he given a library of excellent
books, but he has bequeathed to all who
know the high worth of individual character the legacy of his example and a
spotless reputation.

December 2d, 1859, was the day of the
funeral obsequies ; at one o'clock the
procession, headed by Bishop Potter,
of New York, and the Rev. Dr. Creigh-
ton, the rector of Christ Church, Tarrytown, entered the church ; the pall-
bearers, with the remains of the illustrious dead, followed by numerous
friends of the departed from New
York, Boston, and elsewhere. As the
casket was deposited in front of the

chancel the choir rendered a Gregorian
chant, which was followed by the reading of the usual burial service, after
which the members of the family and a
great company of sorrowing friends
were invited to look for the last time
upon the kindly face of the great author. In that village church there had
never before gathered such groups of
men eminent of letters ; and the vil-
lagers did not forget to exhibit their
emblems of sorrow and sympathy by
draping their houses and closing their
stores. Irving's grave, which is at
Sleepy Hollow Cemetery, is placed in
the centre of the family enclosure, is
marked simply by his name, with the
dates of his birth and death engraved
upon a plain white marble stone.

The scene of the burial was a very
impressive and touching one ; there
were gathered around the open grave a
great concourse of sorrowing friends un-
covered and mute. Never before, perhaps, was there ever witnessed as then
such an illustration of the eloquence of

silence—eulogy or panegyric in this instance was superfluous, since we all well
knew his worth. Thus " Sleepy Hollow," by the possession of this " noble
dust," and by the magic of his charming pen, became invested with a lasting
fame by its association with genius.
His name is, however, enshrined in the
hearts of all lovers of an elevated and
pure literature, while it is also not forgotten in our public places.

It has been justly said that " England
returned him to his native land medalled
by the king, honored by its university,
and followed by the applause of the
whole English people."

George Bancroft fittingly closed his
loving tribute to his noble friend with
these well-chosen words : " There is
the man who during more than fifty
years employed his pen as none other
could have done ; and in all that time
never wrote one word that was tainted
with scepticism, nor one line that was
not as chaste and pure as the violets of
spring." Not only was Irving eminent-

ly gifted with social graces, he was also a genial and enthusiastic lover of nature and all its garniture and glory.

An English writer of excellent books thus speaks of Irving as a " genial, modest, quiet gentleman, averse to all show or flattery and even half averse to fame. There never was any one who so carried the whole of himself in his writings ; the charm of that personal wit and simplicity of character, not without a certain playful subtlety, is never absent. He seldom rises or falls ; he is neither more nor less than himself, and *that* is always delightful, sincere, thorough, and buoyant. He was delightfully desultory and yet capable of sustained effort, as in his ' Life of Washington ' or ' Columbus,' where his heart went with his work."

Mr. Irving has told us that he preferred adopting the mode of short sketches, as affording him greater freedom for the play of sentiment and humor ; and he may be said to have thus introduced a new order of writing.

There is evidence of this, since it at once
attracted the notice of Dickens, whose
" Sketches of Every-day Life" are on
the same model—graphic, fresh, humorous, and picturesque. These writers
alike touched with a master hand the
salient points of the grotesque and hum-
bler ranks of life and brought them into
humorous or ludicrous combinations.
Yet they were not rivals ; their sketches
and portraitures differed in style and detail, and both have achieved a world-wide
fame for having given to us characters
and scenes heretofore unfamiliar, if not
unknown—full of beauty and pathos, as
well as redolent of humor and laughter-
provoking situations.   Dickens, in one
of his genial letters, thus writes to Irving : " I should love to go with you as I
have gone, God knows how often, into
' Little Britain,' ' Eastcheap,' ' Green
Arbor Court,' and ' Westminster Abbey.' I should like to travel with you,
outside of the last of the coaches, down
to ' Bracebridge Hall.' It would make
my heart glad to compare notes with

you about that shabby gentleman in the oil-cloth hat and red nose who sat in the nine-cornered back parlor of the Masons' Arms, and about Robert Preston and the tallow-chandler's widow, whose sitting-room is second nature to me ; and about all those delightful places and people that I used to read about and dream of in the daytime when a very small and not over-particularly taken-care-of boy." Irving may also claim to have been the inventor of Christmas literature, which has, with Dickens and Thackeray, done so much to foster the beautiful in sentiment and feeling connected with that festive, holly-garlanded season of the year.

It has been justly said that " no name in our literature or literary annals is more fondly cherished than that of Washington Irving." One of the earliest and most distinguished of American writers, none has been so generally and heartily loved at home and abroad. This is easily accounted for, since his intellectual gifts were made all the more conspicuous and attractive by the radiancy of his happy and genial temperament.

Among the numerous loving tributes to his memory, Tuckerman has voiced for us one of the best : " No one ever lived a more beautiful life ; no one ever left less to regret in life ; no one ever carried with him to the grave a more universal affection, respect, and sorrow."

The estimate which Mr. Longfellow formed of Mr. Irving in his early days is thus given in one of his letters from Madrid : " Washington Irving is one of those men who put you at ease with them in a moment. He makes no ceremony whatever with one, and, of course, is a very fine man in society—all mirth and good humor." In later days he says : " I had the pleasure of meeting Mr. Irving in Spain, and found the author whom I had loved, repeated in the man ; the same playful humor, the same touches of sentiment, the same poetic atmosphere, and, what I admired still more, the entire absence of all literary jealousy, of all that mean avarice of fame which counts what is given to another as so much taken from one's self :

" And rustling hears in every breeze
The laurels of Miltiades."

At this time Mr. Irving was at Madrid engaged upon his " Life of Columbus ;" and if the work itself did not bear ample testimony to his zealous and conscientious labor, I could do so from personal observation. He seemed to be always at work. " Sit down," he would say, " I will talk with you in a moment ; but I must first finish this sentence." One summer morning, passing his house at the early hour of six, I saw his study window already wide open. On my mentioning it to him afterward he said, " Yes, I am always at my work as early as six." Since then I have often remembered that sunny morning and that open window, so suggestive of his sunny temperament and his open heart, and equally so of his patient and persistent toil.

Mr. Russell Lowell has, in his " Fable

for Critics," so felicitously sketched Irving that his limning seems necessary to an adequate portraiture of our author ; the portrait was made on his return from Madrid :

" Irving ! thrice welcome, warm heart and fine
        brain,
   You bring back the happiest spirit from Spain ;
   And the gravest sweet humor that ever were
        there
   Since Cervantes met death in his gentle despair.

        *   *   *   *   *   *

   So allow me to speak, what I honestly feel,
   To a true-hearted poet, add the fun of Dick
        Steele,
   Throw in all of Addison, minus the chill,
   With the whole of that partnership's stock and
        ' good will,'
   Mix well, and while stirring, hum o'er as a
        spell,
   ' The fine old English gentleman ;' simmer it
        well,
   Sweeten just to your own private liking, then
        strain,
   That only the finest and clearest remain.
   Let it stand out-of-doors till a soul it receives,
   From the warm lazy sun, loitering down through
        green leaves,

And you'll find a choice nature, not wholly de-
    serving
A name either English or Yankee—just Irving."

By his protracted residence abroad, as
well as by his writings, he had succeeded
in dissipating prejudice and linking together in fraternal bonds two great na-
tions more effectively than diplomacy
itself. It should not be forgotten, moreover, that Irving was the first to win for
American letters the respect and recog-
nition of the Old World.

" But the light of his friendly eye is
quenched ; we shall hear no more his
gentle voice nor take his welcome hand.
It is as if some genial year had just
closed and left us in frost and gloom—
its flowery spring, its leafy summer, its
plenteous autumn flown, never to return." * And so, of Sunnyside, now
the shrine of his genius, its glorious attraction has lost much of its magnetic
power—its *genius loci* is gone !

---

* Bryant.

" The dear, quaint cottage, as we pass,
    No clambering rose or ivy hide ;
  But dead leaves fleck the matted grass,
    And *shadow* rests on ' *Sunnyside !* '

  *   *   *   *   *   *

" Yet ne'er did more serene repose
    Of cloud and sunshine, brook and brae,
  Round ' Sleepy Hollow ' fondly close,
    Than on its lover's burial-day !" *

---

* Tuckerman.

HENRY WADSWORTH LONG-FELLOW.

Born 1807, died 1882.

" Oh, deem not 'midst this worldly strife
　An idle art the poet brings,
　Let high philosophy control,
　And sages calm the stream of life ;
'Tis he refines its fountain springs,
　The nobler passions of the soul."

—CAMPBELL.

HENRY WADSWORTH LONG-FELLOW.

AMONG the most pleasant memories of the past was the writer's delightful visit to the poet Longfellow, about a year prior to his lamented death. Few men of letters on either side of the broad Atlantic that it has been his privilege to meet have left such a charm with their names as that of the gifted professor, the subject of the present sketch. During a summer jaunt with a friend to the "modern Athens of America," among its leading objects of interest, historic, artistic, and literary, Craigie House, Cambridge, of course claimed attention—it being not only a shrine of genius, but an historic edifice of storied interest. There are, as is well known, many fascinating attractions that draw the steps of the lover of the picturesque as well as the lover of learning to that classic region—its time-honored halls of learning, its clustered beauties of nature and art, as well as its unrivalled cemetery, Mount Auburn. But the honored name of Longfellow has imparted to that suburban retreat a glory that will linger about Cambridge and Craigie House, by the spell of his muse, that lovers of his beautiful lyrics will enshrine as a perpetual memory.

The writer, as already intimated, had the good fortune to meet the poet in his classic abode, finding him not only in excellent health and spirits, but at leisure. He received his visitors very graciously, and although strangers till then personally, he at once made them feel at ease with him, and readily entered into animated talk about literature and literary persons, their writings, and their respective claims. It is a matter of regret that the substance of his remarks has since passed from memory, now that he has left us and laid aside his lyre forever. Although his voice is silent, his charmed utterances are yet vocal, and are destined to become our common inheritance in the realm of song. Yet even fragments of his words, so gentle and wise, now possess for us a value before unknown. Other poets may cheer and inspire us with their philosophic and ethical teaching ; but Longfellow has imparted to his musical stanzas such a felicitous charm that his productions please all classes and conditions of persons. His generous and even enthusiastic praise of the productions of several of his brother bards was conspicuous as illustrative of his modesty—the modesty of true genius. In this respect he not only resembled Washington Irving, but the analogy holds good as to his kindliness of nature and gentle courtesy of deportment. As the writer entered the house the first object that met his gaze was the old-fashioned *clock on the stairs ;* and passing into the drawing-room, he was cordially received by the host, although his acquaintance with him had hitherto been merely by correspondence. This room was evidently the *sanctum sanctorum* of the poet ; it was decked and garnished with artistic taste, the walls being covered with choice paintings and portraits, while the bookcases were surmounted with statuary and marble busts. On the table and desk at which he usually sat might be noticed many objects of value—rare relics and souvenirs which he had brought from abroad. In fine, this presence chamber looked like a combination of a poet's pleasaunce and an artist's studio.

In course of our conversation an allusion was made to Mr. Ruskin and his great authority as an art critic, to which Mr. Longfellow responded in something like these words : " He resembles a squadron of cavalry, sweeping all before them and taking the field. Ruskin is a master of style," he continued, " and, although not wholly unimpeachable, he is usually correct." When the names were mentioned of James Russell Lowell, Oliver Wendell Holmes, and John Greenleaf Whittier, he did not fail to recognize and applaud their distinctive and characteristic merits. He also referred to the high estimate with which the sage of Concord (Ralph Waldo Emerson) was regarded. It was the writer's good fortune to visit the philosopher in his modest cottage shortly afterward, and to share with him a delightful hour of converse. His aspect was severely simple, quaint, and kindly, and his environment quite in keeping with his personality. Mr. Longfellow took the writer through his apartments and into sundry nooks and corners, in which were to be seen some of his choicest literary treasures. When travelling in Italy, he said he found an incomplete set of Bodoni's celebrated edition of Dante. The set lacked but one volume ; yet, imperfect as it was, he said it was too great a prize to be lost, and so he brought home the volumes. He never dreamed that he should ever find the missing volume ; but, to his joyful surprise, he found it some months after his return home at a

second-hand bookstore in an obscure
street in Boston. His eye lighted up
with evident pleasure and pride as he
exhibited the now completed set. Just
as the writer was leaving, Mr. Longfellow referred to the illustrated edition of
his poems, in two quarto volumes, and
expressed his unqualified pleasure at the
rare excellence of the designs and the
typography. He also mentioned the
fact that such was the scarcity of the
first edition of his poems, that a copy
had been offered for sale at $500. The
home of the poet, many of whose beautiful contributions to our literature are
prized as jewels of our language, and
are of world-wide fame, has been often
described by pen and portrayed by pen-
cil. Like the quaint, picturesque cottage, Sunnyside, Craigie House will long
continue to attract pilgrim feet as a
shrine of genius—one of the "Meccas
of the mind," at which loving tribute
will be offered. This delightful episode
of a summer vacation will not be lost to
memory, that brought the writer face to

face for a brief interval with one of the most gifted and genial of men. In fine, if he may be permitted to cite the words of an eminent English author and tourist, who shared the like pleasure, he would add : "I shall not forget that I have been permitted to touch the hand and to listen to the discourse, full of calm and wise and gentle things, of a noble American gentleman, of him who wrote 'The Psalm of Life,' 'The Village Blacksmith,' and 'Evangeline ;' of him whose life has been blameless, whose record is pure, whose name is a sound of fame to all people." Let us add another noble testimony to his genius from the late John Bright ; his words are the following :

"I do not hesitate to say, as far as my reading has led me to judge, that the 'Song of Hiawatha' is a poem that deserves to live, and will live ; and at this moment it is the finest poem of any language that has been produced by any writer of the United States."

With genius of so high an order, Long-

fellow combined a purity and simplicity
of character rarely excelled or equalled ;
and this it was that won for him so wide
and enduring a fame, as well as such a
cherished regard in the homes of America and Great Britain.   It has been justly remarked that " he was distinguished
for a singular and unfailing love of children and of child life.   At threescore
years and ten he entered into their
thoughts and hopes and sympathies as
if he were yet himself a child.   No man
ever called forth such an expression of
affectionate regard from the hearts of
so many children.   How touching the
incident of the celebration of his birthday, when, on its seventy-second anniversary, the Cambridge schools presented to him a chair made from the wood
of the village blacksmith's chestnut tree.
And how beautiful his verses of acknowl-
edgment from " The Arm-Chair :"

" And thus, dear children, have ye made for me
    this day a jubilee ;
  And to my more than threescore years and ten
    brought back my youth again.

Only your love and your remembrance could
    give life to this dead wood,
And make these branches—leafless now so long
    —blossom again in song."

Longfellow was emphatically the poet of his native land. Though deeply imbued with the classic spirit, and revelling at his ease in all the treasures of English and European literature, the scenery and art of the Old World, with its mighty monuments and ancient historic memories, his heart was yet in this New World—its wild scenes and its fresh life ; and here he found a home for his muse, and he made that home illustrious. He has shown us that the spirit of poesy resides here as well as there.

" Thy song shall speak to old and young,
    While song yet speaks an English tongue,
        By Charles' or Thames' wave."

Longfellow wrote his " Hyperion," which followed his " Outre Mer," in 1839, and it at once met with general acceptation, being of that charming order —travel books—which wins by its literary attractions. "The Psalm of Life" and many of his well-known lyrics followed in quick succession, of which, to cite the words of one of his brother bards, it may be said that "they are delicate renderings of our common emotions ; and there is a humanity in them which is irresistible in the fit measures to which they are wedded. If some elegiac poets have strung rosaries of tears, there is a weakness of woe in their verses which repels ; but the quiet, pensive thought, the twilight of the mind, in which the little facts of life are saddened in view of their relation to the eternal laws, time and change, this is the meditation and mourning of every manly heart ; and this is the alluring and permanent charm of Longfellow's poetry."

Longfellow's modesty may be seen in his impromptu on a certain occasion, when, on being introduced to Mr. Longworth, who happened to meet him in company, "I am happy to meet you, Mr. Longworth," said the professor, "for it reminds me of the adage :

" Worth makes the man—the want of it, the
    fellow ;
And all the rest is leather and prunella."

It seems quite superfluous to cite
stanzas that chime in almost every person's memory ; yet for the very few who
may not have seen them, the following
are given :

" Lives of great men all remind us
    We can make our lives sublime,
And, departing, leave behind us
    Footprints on the sands of time—

" Footprints, that perhaps another,
    Sailing o'er life's solemn main,
A forlorn and shipwrecked brother,
    Seeing, shall take heart again."

" No endeavor is in vain—
    Its reward is in the doing ;
    And the rapture of pursuing
Is the prize the vanquished gain."

" All are architects of fate,
    Working in these walls of time ;
Some with massive deeds and great,
    Some with ornaments of rhyme.

" In the elder days of art,
　　Builders wrought with greatest care
　Each minute and unseen part ;
　　For the gods see everywhere.

" Let us do our work as well,
　　Both the unseen and the seen ;
　Make the house where gods may dwell
　　Beautiful, entire and clean.''

And this little gem, written as he neared his eighth decade :

" Is it too late ? Ah, nothing is too late
Till the tired heart shall cease to palpitate.''
" Something remains for us to do or dare,
Even the oldest tree some fruit may bear ;
For age gives opportunity, no less
Than youth itself, tho' in another dress,
And as the evening twilight fades away
The sky is filled with stars, invisible by day.''

In his diary, under date of December 6th, 1838, Professor Longfellow wrote these words : " A beautiful, holy morning within me. I was softly excited. I knew not why, and wrote with peace in my heart, and not without tears in my eyes, ' The Reaper and the Flowers : a Psalm of Death.' I have had an idea of this kind in my mind for a long time without finding any expression for it in words. This morning it seemed to crystallize at once, without any effort of my own." His biographer thus relates the one great tragedy that left its traces on the gentle and beautiful life of the poet : " There is a break in the journal here ; and then these lines of Tennyson, added many days after :

" Sleep sweetly, tender heart, in peace !
    Sleep, holy spirit, blessed soul !
  While the stars burn, the moons increase,
    And the great ages onward roll."

· This break in the journal marked a break in his very life. His wife was sitting in the library with her two little girls engaged in sealing up some small packages of their curls which she had just cut off. From a match fallen upon the floor her light summer dress caught fire. The shock was too great, and she died the next morning. Three days later her burial took place at Mount Auburn—it was the anniversary of her marriage day. Eighteen years after he wrote the commemorative, touching lines, " The Cross of Snow," found in his portfolio after his death.

Longfellow's character as a poet seems to us one of graceful symmetry in its fertility of imagination, affluence of thought, and picturesqueness of its diction ; and the world has fully recognized his claim to a prominent niche in the temple of fame. The lesson of his literary life has much in it for the head and heart to ponder ; it was a healthful and an elevated one well worthy of being studied.

When he visited England he was received with every expression of regard ; it was, indeed, the hearty greeting of affection paid to a long-loved and honored friend. A life which has been crowned with such abundant fruitage, such a revenue of noble teaching enshrined in the music of speech, must have been a devoted and laborious one. He has himself given us an insight into the secret of his success as a philosophic poet in the closing stanza of his " Voices of the Night :"

> " Look, then, into thine heart and write !
>   Yes, into Life's deep stream !
>   All forms of sorrow and delight—
>   All solemn voices of the night,
>   That can soothe thee, or affright—
>   Be these henceforth thy theme !"

Thus we hear his " Psalm of Life" repeated by boys at college, grave statesmen in Congress or Parliament, and even more sympathetically at the fireside. The world has been not only enriched by the genius of Longfellow—it has been made better.

His famous poem " Excelsior" has a history. One night, after the poet had attended a party of friends, he took up a New York newspaper having the arms of the State—a shield with a rising sun, and the motto, " Excelsior." This attracted his notice, and the word suggested the poem, which was an impromptu, and was written on the back of a letter of his friend, Charles Sumner. Like his other beautiful lyric,

" The Footsteps of Angels"—the one a hymn of aspiration, the other a hymn of patience—both will live among the immortals of song. After Longfellow's visit to Europe, in 1868, where he became the honored guest of the literary celebrities abroad, he received the academic degree of D.C.L. from the University of Oxford ; the queen sent for him, and the poet, in the usual republican fashion, shook her majesty by the hand—a familiarity not accorded to her liege subjects.

With these charming stanzas closes this tribute :

" Spake full well, in language quaint and olden,
    One who dwelleth by the castled Rhine,
When he called the flowers, so blue and golden,
    Stars, that in earth's firmament do shine.

" Stars they are, wherein we read our history,
    As astrologers and seers of eld ;
Yet not wrapped about with awful mystery,
    Like the burning stars, which they beheld.

" Wondrous truths, and manifold as wondrous,
    God hath written in those stars above ;
But not less in the bright flowerets under us
    Stands the revelation of his love.

" Not alone in meadows and green alleys,
  On the mountain-top and by the brink
Of sequestered pools in woodland valleys,
  Where the slaves of Nature stoop to drink ;

" Not alone in her vast dome of glory,
  Not on graves of bird and beast alone,
But in old cathedrals, high and hoary,
  On the tombs of heroes, carved in stone ;

" In the cottage of the rudest peasant,
  In ancestral homes, whose crumbling towers,
Speaking of the Past unto the Present,
  Tell us of the ancient games of Flowers ;

" In all places, then, and in all seasons,
  Flowers expand their light and soul-like
    wings,
Teaching us, by most persuasive reasons,
  How akin they are to human things.

" And with child-like, credulous affection
  We behold their tender buds expand,
Emblems of our own great resurrection,
  Emblems of the bright and better land."

I, nearer to the Wayside Inn
Where toil shall cease and rest begin,
  Am weary, thinking of your road.
O little hands ! that weak or strong
Have still to serve or rule so long,
  Have still so long to give or ask ;
I, who so much with book and pen
Have toiled among my fellow-men,
  Am weary, thinking of your task.
O little hearts ! that throb and beat
With such impatient, feverish heat,
  Such limitless and strong desires ;
Mine, that so long has glow'd and burn'd,
With passions into ashes turn'd,
  Now covers and conceals its fires.
O little souls ! as pure and white
And crystalline as rays of light,
  Direct from Heaven, their source divine ;
Refracted through the mist of years,
How red my setting sun appears,
  How lurid looks this soul of mine !"

WILLIAM CULLEN BRYANT.

Born 1797, died 1878.

"While he is best known by his poems, Mr. Bryant is considered by the best authorities one of the finest prose writers in the country. He was distinctively a student and interpreter of Nature ; all her aspects and voices were familiar to him, and are reproduced in his poetry."

—G. R. CATHCART.

WILLIAM CULLEN BRYANT.

An accepted authority * has said that "a true poet, a man in whose heart resides some effluence of wisdom, some tone of the 'eternal melodies,' is the most precious gift that can be bestowed on a generation. We see in him a freer, purer development of whatever is noblest in ourselves ; his life is a rich lesson to us, and we mourn his death as that of a benefactor who loved and taught us." In harmony with this is the graceful estimate of Washington Irving, whose words are these : "A poet, of all writers, has the best chance for immortality ; others may write from the head, but he writes from the heart, and the heart will always understand him. His

---

* Carlyle.

writings, therefore, contain the spirit, the aroma of the age in which he lives. They are caskets which enclose within a small compass the wealth of the language—its family jewels, which are thus transmitted in a portable form to posterity." Much also has been claimed for the true poet, whose musical utterances not only elevate and refine those who would not be taught the lessons of life in stern didactic prose, but because the gems of poesy, which are recognized as classics of artistic beauty, "bring pleasure to millions of the human race, like the sunshine of the morning after the shadows of night flee away." Mr. Bryant himself has said that "the elements of poetry lie in natural objects, in the vicissitudes of common life, in the emotions of the heart and in the relations of society." As Bryant's name has long been recognized as one of the representative poets of our country, it may be proper to glance back to the time when he first became a citizen of its metropolitan city. Mr. Bryant's life-

time may be said to have been coeval
with the great formative and progressive
development of the republic—scientific,
political, and literary.

It is, indeed, not one of the least of
the distinctive glories of this country
that it has not only demonstrated the
feasibility of popular government, but
that it has also taken the lead in popular education, and has had an ample
share in the triumphs of inventive and
scientific discovery. Within the limits
of a lifetime its progress and proficiency
in the several departments of learning
are among the marvels of an age itself
one of unparalleled achievements.

Mr. Bryant, like Professor Longfellow, traced his ancestry back to the
memorable landing of the Mayflower.
From his early days he seems to have
caught poetic fire from his favorites—
Pope, Wordsworth, Gray, and Goldsmith. Indeed, he wrote verses at the
age of ten, and when at the age of eighteen years he produced his "Thanatopsis" (view of death), which at once won

for him the laurel chaplet of fame. It was at the suggestion of a legal friend that he left his native Berkshire Hills and came to New York to study and practise law ; but he did not succeed in that profession, for his preference, it was soon evident, was for Wordsworth rather than for Blackstone. He accordingly devoted himself to literature, and at about thirty-two years of age he became associate editor with Mr. Coleman, the editor of the *Evening Post*, then one of the leading organs of political thought. His name had subsequently been connected with that journal until within a few years of his death. But Mr. Bryant is best known to us as the poet who has sought his inspiration from American forests, mountains and rivers, as well as the feathered minstrels and the varied aspects of Nature in her leafy garniture and grandeur. For example, of his descriptive verse, these opening stanzas "To the Evening Wind" are cited :

" Spirit that breathest through my lattice, thou
That cool'st the twilight of the sultry day,

Gratefully flows thy freshness round my brow ;
Thou hast been out upon the deep at play,
Riding all day the wild blue waves till now,
Roughening their crests, and scattering high
    their spray,
And swelling the white sail. I welcome thee
To the scorch'd land, thou wanderer of the sea !

" Nor I alone ; a thousand bosoms round
Inhale thee in the fulness of delight ;
And languid forms rise up, and pulses bound
Livelier, at coming of the wind of night ;
And languishing, to hear thy grateful sound,
Lies the vast inland stretched beyond the sight.
Go forth into the gathering shade ; go forth,
God's blessing breathed upon the fainting earth !

" Go, rock the little wood-bird in his nest,
Curl the still waters, bright with stars, and
    rouse
The wild old wood from his majestic rest,
Summoning from the innumerable boughs
The strange deep harmonies that haunt his
    breast :
Pleasant shall be thy way, where meekly bows
The shutting flower, and darkling waters pass,
And where the o'ershadowing branches sweep
    the grass."

When the pioneer effort was being
made by the writer, seeking the enact-

ment of an international copyright treaty between the United States and Great Britain, it was that he first met Mr. Bryant. Like Irving, Lowell, Longfellow, Bancroft, Motley, Whittier, and many other eminent writers, Bryant attached his name to several petitions to Congress in behalf of the measure. In addition to these, there was also presented a " Memorial" of fifty-six British authors—comprising the most distinguished writers of that day—who signed the document. This interesting manuscript —which was procured by Messrs. Saunders & Otley, the London publishers, and by them consigned to the care of Captain Wilkes, of the United States Exploring Expedition—was, on his arrival here, delivered to the writer. It was then duly forwarded to Henry Clay, who presented it to the Senate of the United States.

When Charles Dickens first visited this country, he at once became interested in and co-operated with the enterprise ; and an American petition to Congress was prepared by the writer, signed by the most prominent authors of the time, which document Mr. Dickens took with him to Washington and handed personally to Hon. Henry Clay. In response, autograph letters from the illustrious statesman and the distinguished novelist came in due course. But to return from this digression to the subject of our sketch—the poet.

In his apostrophe to the " Fringed Gentian" we have a graceful illustration of Bryant's ethical muse :

" Thou comest not when violets lean
    O'er wandering brooks and springs unseen,
    Or columbines, in purple drest,
    Nod o'er the ground-bird's hidden nest.
    Thou waitest late and com'st alone,
    When woods are bare and birds are flown,
    And frosts and shortening days portend
    The aged year is near his end.
    Then doth thy sweet and quiet eye
    Look through its fringes to the sky—
    Blue—blue—as if that sky let fall
    A flower from its cerulean wall.
    I would that thus, when I shall see
    The hour of death draw near to me,

Hope blossoming within my heart—
May look to heaven as I depart."

He was invited to write a patriotic poem for the semi-centennial anniversary of the New York Historical Society. The poem formed four stanzas, beginning :

" Great were the hearts and strong the minds
Of those who framed in high debate
The immortal league of Love that binds
Our fair, broad empire, State with State."

Mr. Bryant was a wonderful worker ; not only was his editorial industry remarkable, but his contributions to our American literature, both in prose and verse, afford abundant evidence of the fact. He was an accomplished student of the literature of many languages, and while his translations from other tongues are so felicitous that his fellow-master, Longfellow, praised some of his Spanish translations as rivalling the originals in beauty, yet his own verse is as free from merely literary influence or reminiscence as the pure air of his native hills from the perfume of exotics. His last considerable poem, " The Flood of Years," but echoes in its meditative flow the solemn cadences of " Thanatopsis." One stanza—perhaps the most familiar if not the best in all his verse—will long be the climax of patriotic appeal :

" Truth, crushed to earth, shall rise again ;
  The eternal years of God are hers ;
  But Error, wounded, writhes with pain,
  And dies among his worshippers."

Bryant made his fifth voyage to Europe in 1857, travelling in Spain and Algiers ; and after his return he published a volume of " Letters from Spain." He went again abroad in 1865 and 1867, making in all seven visits to the Old World. Although many persons might suppose the poet, from the tenor of much of his writings, to have been of a grave and ascetic tendency, the following extract from one of his letters, written in 1863, proves that he was not devoid of humor, and even that of a rollicksome mood. In his letter to the Rev. Dr. Dewey, he says :

" Looking at your last a second time, it strikes me that you might, perhaps, expect that I should answer some part of it. Let me say, then, that we will give you a reasonable time to consider the question of coming to Roslyn, you and Mrs. Dewey, if you will only come at last, and before the days arrive described in the verses which you will find on the other leaf of this sheet :

" The season wears an aspect glum and glummer ;
The icy north wind, an unwelcome comer,
Frighting from garden-walks each pretty hum-
    mer,
Whose murmuring music lulled the noons of
    summer,
Roars in the woods, with grummer voice and
    grummer,
And thunders in the forest like a drummer.
Dumb are the birds—they could not well be
    dumber.

" The winter cold, life's pitiless benumber,
Bursts water-pipes, and makes us call the
    plumber ;
Now, by the fireside, toils the patient thumber
Of ancient books, and no less patient summer
Of long accounts ; while topers fill the rummer,

The maiden thinks what furs will best become
    her,
And on the stage-boards shouts the gibing
    mummer.
Shut in by storms, the dull piano strummer
Murders old tunes — there's nothing weari-
    somer !"

Mr. Bryant's presence was an impressive one ; his venerable aspect in his
later years gave him a picturesque and
striking appearance. His simple and
natural mode of rural life doubtless
tended to counteract the effects upon his
physical frame caused by his unremit-
ting mental labor as editor and poet.
The personal friend of Dr. Dewey and
Dr. Bellows, the Unitarian clergymen of
New York, and an attendant upon their
ministry ; yet no one ever recognized
more completely nor more devoutly the
divinity of Christ.* To a little volume
from the pen of the Rev. Dr. Alden, en-
titled "Thoughts on the Religious
Life," he contributed a preface, in
which he says : "I cannot but lament

---

* John Bigelow's Memoirs.

the tendency of the time, encouraged by some in the zealous prosecution of science, to turn its attention from the teachings of the Gospel, from the beautiful examples of Christ's life and the supremely excellent precepts which He gave to His disciples and the people who resorted to hear Him. To those teachings and that example the world owes its recovery from the abominations of heathenism. . . . I tremble to think what the world would be without Him. Take away the blessing of the advent of His life and the blessings purchased by His death, in what an abyss of guilt would man have been left! It would seem to be blotting the sun out of the heavens, to leave our system of worlds in chaos, frost, and darkness. In my view of the life, the teachings, the labors, and the sufferings of the blessed Jesus, there can be no admiration too profound, no love of which the human heart is capable too warm, no gratitude too earnest and deep of which He is justly the object." This admirable testimony was believed to have been among the last things that Mr. Bryant wrote.

Like Irving, whenever an occasion called for it, he was the coveted guest at public gatherings, celebrations, and banquets ; and both suffered from modest diffidence when called upon for a speech. Bryant's tenacity of memory was phenomenal. Pope and Words-worth seem to have been his favorites, and also Johnson's " Lives of the Poets." His love of literary work and ability to labor continued almost to the close of his career ; and even in his great work, the translation of Homer, he evinced no lack of intellectual skill or indication of senility.

Mr. John Bigelow, in his able memoir of the poet, remarks that " he was not a man of moods and tenses, and that his seasons for productive labor did not alternate like the seasons of the calendar year, or the ebb and flow of the tides. ' I cannot say,' he wrote to a gentleman who had addressed him some inquiries upon the subject, ' that in writing my poems I am directly conscious of the action of an outside intelligence ; but I sometimes wonder whence the thoughts come, and they seem to me hardly my own. Sometimes, in searching for the adequate expression, it seems suddenly darted into my mind like a ray of light into a dark room, and gives me a kind of surprise. I don't invoke the muse at all. It appears to me that inspiration has no more to do with one intellectual process than another, and that if there is such a thing, it might be present as directly in the solutions of a problem of high mathematics, as in a copy of verses.' ''

The writer well remembers meeting the poet one wintry morning as he was on his way from his rural home at Roslyn to the office of the *Evening Post* in New York. In his reply to the remark that it seemed strange that he did not stay in the city during the austerity of winter, he said that he gloried in the winter's landscape, with its snow-clad aspects, as much as in the radiant summer, with its sunshine and its flowers.

In his poem styled " A Winter Piece"
are some lines confirmatory of this :

" But Winter has yet brighter scenes—he boasts
  Splendors beyond what gorgeous Summer
      knows—
  Or Autumn, with his many fruits, and woods
  All flushed with many hues. Come when the
      rains
  Have glazed the snow, and clothed the trees
      with ice ;
  While the slant sun of February pours
  Into the bowers a flood of light. Approach !"

The following lines are addressed to
the " Autumn Woods":

    " Ere, in the northern gale,
The summer tresses of the trees are gone,
The woods of autumn, all around our vale
        Have put their glory on.

    " The mountains that infold,
In their wide sweep, the colored landscape round,
Seem groups of giant kings, in purple and gold,
        That guards the enchanted ground.

    " I roam the woods that crown
The upland, where the mingled splendors glow,
Where the gay company of trees look down
        On the green fields below.

" My steps are not alone
In these bright walks ; the sweet southwest, at play,
Flies, rustling, where the painted leaves are strown
    Along the winding way.

" Oh, Autumn ! why so soon
Depart the hues that make thy forests glad :
Thy gentle wind and thy fair, sunny noon,
    And leave thee wild and sad !"

Take yet another extract of his pastoral poetry, " The Prairies :"

" These are the Gardens of the Desert, these
    The unshorn fields, boundless and beautiful,
    For which the speech of England has no name—
    The Prairies.   I behold them for the first,
    And my heart swells, while the dilated sight
    Takes in the encircling vastness.   Lo ! they
        stretch
    In airy undulations, far away,
    As if the ocean, in his gentlest swell,
    Stood still, with all his rounded billows fixed,
    And motionless forever.   Motionless ?—
    No—they are all unchained again.   The clouds
    Sweep over with their shadows, and, beneath,
    The surface rolls and fluctuates to the eye ;
    Dark hollows seem to glide along and chase
    The sunny ridges.   Breezes of the South !"

Like Wordsworth's, Bryant's muse
evidently loved to commune with Nature

in her solitary grandeur, her forests, hills, and streams.

With the demands of journalism and the devotion to the muse—indeed, his seems to have been a kind of dual life.

Although so familiar to most readers of poetic literature, it may be admissible, perhaps, here to cite the first and last stanzas of his " Thanatopsis" :

" To him who in the love of Nature holds
Communion with her visible forms, she speaks
A various language ; for his gayer hours
She has a voice of gladness, and a smile
And eloquence of beauty, and she glides
Into his darker musings with a mild
And healing sympathy, that steals away
Their sharpness ere he is aware.

* * * * *

" As the long train
Of ages glides away, the sons of men—
The youth in life's green spring, and he who
goes
In the full strength of years, matron and maid,
And the sweet babe, and the gray-headed man—
Shall one by one be gathered to thy side,
By those who, in their turn, shall follow them.
So live that, when thy summons comes to join
The innumerable caravan that moves

To that mysterious realm where each shall take
His chamber in the silent halls of death—
Thou go, not like the quarry-slave at night,
Scourged to his dungeon, but sustained and
    soothed
By an unfaltering trust, approach thy grave,
Like one who wraps the drapery of his couch
About him, and lies down to pleasant dreams."

Mr. Bryant's last printed poem, on "Washington's Birthday," of which these are the closing stanzas, has been much admired :

" Lo where beneath an icy shield
    Calmly the mighty Hudson flows !
By snow-clad fell and frozen field
    Broadening the mighty river goes.

" The wildest storm that sweeps through space,
    And rends the oak with sudden force,
Can raise no ripple on his face,
    Or slacken his majestic course.

" Thus 'mid the wreck of thrones shall live
    Unmarred, undimmed our hero's fame,
And years succeeding years shall give
    Increase of honors to his name."

His closing days seemed to be under the shadow of unconsciousness. After his delivery of an address at the unveil-

ing of a statue to the memory of the
Italian patriot, Mazzini, in Central Park,
New York, in the spring of 1878, having
too freely exposed himself to the heat of
the sun, he became suddenly unconscious, and fell. This superinduced a
comatose condition, in which state he
lingered about two weeks, when his
kindly presence left us in great sorrow.

In the glowing words of one eminent
in the world of letters, it may be well to
now sum up this tribute to his memory,
since the generous and eloquent estimate finds a cordial response in the personal recollections of the writer : '' During all these busy years he had become
a man of threescore and ten. The pleasant city that he knew when he came to
New York was now the chief city of the
Western continent—one of the great
cities of the world ; and the poet, whose
immortal distinction it was to have written the first memorable American poem,
and whose fame was part of the national
glory—the editor who, with perfect un-
selfishness and unswerving fidelity, had

expounded and defended great funda-
mental principles of national progress
and prosperity, became our patriarch,
our mentor, our most conspicuous citizen.   Every movement of art and literature, of benevolence and good citizen-
ship, sought the decoration of his name.
His presence was the grace of every fes-
tival, and although he had always instinctively shrunk from personal public-
ity, he yielded to a fate benignant for
the community.   From his childhood
and through all his eighty-four years
his habits of life were temperate and
careful.   He rose early, took active exercise, spared work at night, yet had time
for every duty of a fully occupied life,
and at seventy-one sat down in the
shadow of the great sorrow of his life,
to seek a wise distraction, in translat-
ing the ' Iliad ' and the ' Odyssey.'   No
man ever bore the burden of years more
lightly.   The primeval woods, ' God's
first temples,' breathe the solemn bene-
diction of his verse." *

---

* G. W. Curtis.

JOSEPH GREEN COGSWELL.

Born 1786, died 1871.

" Blest with a taste exact, yet unconfined ;
A knowledge both of books and human kind ;
Generous converse, a soul exempt from pride
Ready to praise, with reason on his side ;
Careless of censure, nor too fond of fame ;
Averse to flatter, yet not apt to blame."

—POPE.

JOSEPH GREEN COGSWELL.*

THE age in which we are living is a privileged one, being characterized by intense intellectual activity throughout the civilized world. It is almost superfluous to add that this is seen, not only in its unprecedented number of writers and readers, but also in the marvellous multiplication of the higher institutions of learning, free public libraries, and academies of art and science, as well as our ubiquitous·common schools.

The time-honored foundations of learning in the Old World, until recently, were accessible to comparatively few privileged scientists and scholars ; but these restrictions have at length been

---

* This paper was prepared at request of and read before the International Conference of Librarians in the autumn of 1887, and afterward printed in their *Library Journal.*

abandoned, and the temples of science and literature are now made universally available. In a country of such free political institutions as ours, moral and intellectual culture is a necessity, and may even be said to be the palladium of our perpetuity as a nation. While these invaluable auxiliaries for the promotion of the highest interests of the people are thus so characteristic of our day, it is fitting that we hold in cherished esteem the memory of the self-denying and the devoted services of those who have been conspicuously among its pioneers, in the planning and developing of the grand movement, and foremost, perhaps, among them was the subject of this sketch.

Joseph Green Cogswell, as to his ancestral history, came of Puritan origin—his progenitor, John Cogswell, having left Bristol, England, in 1635, and settled in Ipswich, Mass., where many of his descendants long continued to reside. The subject of our memoir was graduated at Harvard in 1806, and shortly afterward he made a voyage to India. On his return to New York, he studied law with Fisher Ames and subsequently entered upon the practice of the profession at Belfast, Me. It was for a short time only, however, he preferring to be a tutor at Cambridge. In 1812 he was married to Mary, daughter of Governor Gilman, of New Hampshire. The union was soon dissolved, as she died of consumption the following year. In 1816 he joined his. friends, Edward Everett and George Ticknor, in making a trip to Europe, and while at the leading capitals abroad, he paid especial attention to the methods and principles of instruction. He remained in Europe about four years, spending considerable time at Göttingen for this purpose.

On his return home, in 1820, he became Professor of Mineralogy and Geology in Harvard College, and also its Librarian. In 1823, in company with George Bancroft, the historian, he founded the Round Hill School at Northampton, Mass., on the plan of the

German and English academies. This
institution attracted to itself many stu-
dents from all parts of the United States,
and exerted an important influence in
advancing the standard of education
among us. Mr. Cogswell afterward
established a similar school at Raleigh,
N. C. Three years later he returned to
New York, and became the editor of
what was then regarded as the leading
critical periodical, the New York *Review ;* it was continued to ten volumes.
It may here be stated that the professor
during his European travels had enjoyed
the acquaintance of many of the most
illustrious men of letters—Goethe, Humboldt, Béranger, Byron, Scott, Jeffrey,
and many more. In 1839 he was introduced by Fitz-Greene Halleck to Mr.
John Jacob Astor. At this early date,
the millionaire contemplated, it is said,
the founding of some public institution
in the city of his adoption—New York.
The first suggestion of the establishment
of a free public library has been, by
some persons, attributed to Washington

Irving, and by others to Mr. Cogswell ; but he has himself stated that '' it was a kind impulse of Mr. Astor's own heart which prompted him to the establishment of some permanent and valuable memorial to testify his grateful feelings toward the city in which he had so long lived and prospered.''

From the best of our means of information on the subject, it appears that Mr. Astor, being somewhat undecided as to the particular form his bequest should assume, Mr. Cogswell urged the importance of a Public Library of Reference. Both Mr. Irving and Mr. Brevoort coincided in the view. During the closing years of Mr. Astor's life Mr. Cogswell was in daily attendance upon him, as his companion, and in pursuance of the determination of founding a library, he was authorized by him to begin preparations for the work. Mr. Cogswell devoted himself accordingly to the planning and preparatory service. Although Mr. Irving, who was also Mr. Astor's frequent guest, sug-

gested that it would be a good thing for
him at once to put into execution his
noble enterprise, yet it was left to be
carried out under the provisions of his
will.   Having thus been entrusted with
the management of the design, the collecting of the books commenced.   The
first collection of works were about one
thousand volumes, including Mr. Astor's copy of Audubon's great work on
" American Ornithology," in four large
folio volumes.   In 1842, when Mr. Washington Irving was appointed United
States Minister to the Court of Spain,
he desired to have Mr. Cogswell accompany him as Secretary to the Lega-
tion.

    In writing to the authorities at Wash-
ington, Irving thus refers to his friend :
" He is a gentleman with whom I am on
terms of confidential intimacy, and I
know no one who, by his various ac-
quirements, his prompt sagacity, his
knowledge of the world, his habits of
business and his obliging disposition, is
so calculated to give me counsel, aid,

and companionship, so important in Madrid, where a stranger is more isolated than in any other capital of Europe."

Just as he had succeeded in procuring this appointment, Mr. Astor heard of it, and finding that he was likely to lose his valuable services for the projected library, he at once made Mr. Cogswell its librarian. In 1848, after the death of Mr. Astor, the librarian was sent to Europe to purchase books ; meanwhile the preparations were in progress for the erection of the building. Returning from his tour, he brought home about twenty thousand volumes, chiefly selected from the marts of London and Paris. These books were deposited in a house 32 Bond Street, hired for the purpose. The writer called there on the bibliographer more than once. On entering the parlors, he found him with his hands full of books ; books piled up on his table ; the floor so covered with books that he did not know where to move ; the walls were also garnished with books. Whichever way the eye turned there

were books—books to the right of him,
books to the left of him, books in the
rear and books to the front of him.

The act of incorporation of the library
took effect January, 1849. The officers
were eleven trustees, Mr. Irving being
president, Mr. William B. Astor treas-
urer, and Mr. Cogswell the superintendent.

In 1850 he was instructed to make another visit to Europe for the purchase
of books to the extent of $25,000.
While in Paris he was aided by Hector
Bossange, then the leading bookseller
and bibliopolist. Meanwhile, Mr. Cogswell had prepared and had printed an
alphabetical catalogue of books essential
to the completion of a cosmopolitan
library. This valuable manual, which
was the product of great skill and labor,
is now scarce, and has been known to
sell for $5. He visited the literary cen-
tres of Paris, London, Brussels, and
Berlin, and there being at the time some
important auction sales pending, he was
enabled to buy many rare and valuable

works at a great reduction of cost. Later on he made another trip abroad, remaining several months there, and visiting the most important book-marts, from Rôme on the south to Stockholm on the north. His collections now were of the first importance, comprising most of the rare and valuable productions that have since imparted its distinctive character of excellence to the library.

As illustrative of the bibliographical skill and critical acumen displayed by the superintendent in his selections, he might quote the words of Mr. Burton in his " Book-Hunter," where he says : " In the Astorian Library the selections of books have been made with great judgment ; innate literary value being held an object more important than mere abstract rarity." The numerical extent of the collection at this time was eighty thousand volumes ; and even at that early day similar high estimates of its value were expressed by several other eminent scholars abroad, Humboldt, Bunsen, and Lepsius being among the number.   The establishment of a great free library on the plan of the Astor was here not only a novelty, it was also a prophecy of the transformation it was destined to effect in the social condition of the metropolis.   It is due to the memory of Dr. Cogswell to add that it was to his eminent attainments as a linguist, and to his sagacious forethought that the success of the great enterprise is mainly to be ascribed.   The works which his diligent search and wise economy secured were of the class which are now required by the professional writer and student, and which in some instances even to this day are unattainable elsewhere on this continent.

It was during the ten years' interval between his appointment as librarian and the collecting of the books from abroad that the doctor devoted himself so assiduously to the preparatory labors that resulted so successfully in the development of the library.   Dr. Cogswell made in all six voyages to Europe, four for the purchasing of books for the library. And it may be proper here to cite the testimony of a person himself conversant with books, who states that "No library in the land was founded with more discrimination and economy ; the books purchased to-day would sell for ten times the amount that was expended for them, while many of them cannot now be bought at any price."

In January, 1854, Dr. Cogswell formally opened the Astor Library, ten days being devoted to the exhibition of its rare and costly works of art.

In two years, when the first building was found to be crowded to its utmost capacity, the volumes amounting to about one hundred thousand, Mr. William B. Astor, son of the founder, erected a second hall adjoining the original structure, and uniform in style with it. During the erection of the new building Dr. Cogswell undertook the arduous and self-imposed task of preparing and superintending the printing of the alphabetical catalogue of the library, forming four large octavo volumes. In addition

to this herculean labor, he had to super-
intend the routine service of the library
as well as its entire rearrangement and
classification. He also gave to the
library his own valuable and complete
collection of works on bibliography in
many languages, extending to over five
thousand volumes.

It was after Dr. Cogswell had completed a supplemental volume, the fifth
of his catalogue, that his physical
strength visibly declined, although his
mental vigor remained unimpaired, and
he felt it his duty to tender to the Board
of Trustees his resignation. After about
a score of years devoted to its interests
he left the library with regret, and he
evinced his loving regard for its success
by his subsequent visits. In accepting
his official resignation the trustees recorded their high sense of his valuable
services in words profoundly expressive
of their grateful esteem and regret at
losing their continuance.

In the central hall of the library are
two marble busts — one facing the en-

trance is that of the honored founder, and at the western end that of Dr. Cogswell, the superintendent. It is an admirable likeness, and was the work of Lequesne, of Paris, whose decorations of the Louvre and the tomb of Napoleon at the Invalides have rendered his name famous. In the south, or original hall, is a marble bust of Washington Irving, the first president of the institution.

Having thus briefly sketched the leading events of his literary career, it may not be inappropriate to add a few words respecting his personal character. This may be seen at a glance in the loving regard of his pupils at the Round Hill School, long after they had taken their devious ways in life ; and no less in the cordial testimonial of his associates in the Board of Trustees. Nor was his devoted service to the library unappreciated by the estimable family it represents. And were it needed to extend the testimony, I might add that, having been for several years his official assistant, it affords the writer much pleasure to state that during those years he remembers only his uniform kindliness and refined courtesy of deportment.   Although having had the *entrée* of the coteries of literary and fashionable life in Paris, London, and Berlin, as well as the best society here, he was yet remarkable for his urbane and suave deportment, without the least ostentation.

Dr. Cogswell received his honorary degree of LL.D. from Trinity in 1842, and the distinction was again conferred by Harvard in 1863.   Like other men of genius, Dr. Cogswell had his harmless eccentricities ; one was his ·refusal to wear an overcoat, even in the coldest weather ; and he was never seen to seek shelter from the rain under an umbrella.   He was simple in his dress and generally also in his diet, and if his average health and longevity are considered, he proved the good effects of the latter.   His memory was remarkably tenacious, especially in whatever concerned the books of the library.   He was not an infrequent guest at the table of Mr. William B. Astor when he resided in Lafayette Place, and on one occasion, a question occurred in the conversation, concerning some place on the African coast, and it not being satisfactorily answered, Mr. Washington Irving being present, said, "Ask Cogswell ; he knows everything." The doctor responded that he knew the particular spot, having been sent as supercargo of a vessel to that coast.

Longfellow thus incidentally refers to his having visited him : "Dr. Cogswell is here, and is truly a god-send." He was not only a scholar of wide scope, having a knowledge of classic, Oriental, Scandinavian, Slavic, and other European and Asiatic literature ; he was also a Christian, as the following interesting extract from one of his letters evinces : "God has never given me over to unbelief. At no period of my life has a doubt arisen in my mind in regard to the great spiritual truths—God the Creator, Christ the Redeemer, the Holy

Spirit the Sanctifier are realities with me as much as the earth upon which I tread.   I would not give up this belief for the gift of the greatest intellect, the highest rank, or the most unbounded wealth ever attained by mortal man. . . . I believe in the reality of a future life as fully as I believe in the present."

It is pleasant to notice, in the following extracts from his later correspondence, the indications of his happy temperament and calm state of mind, when his physical strength was abating, he writes at the close of 1865 thus to a friend : " I have great cause for gratitude to God.   As He brings me nearer and nearer to the close of life, He grants me as much freedom from the usual trials of old age as its condition ever allows, and more of its comforts than I could reasonably expect.   In a social point of view, it is true I lose a good deal from impaired hearing ; on the other hand, I am spared hearing an infinite deal of nonsense.   My eyesight is still good, and I look upon the beauties of nature and art with as much, if not more delight than ever, and enjoy a greater serenity of mind than I did when my cares were more distracting.   Above all, as my sun nears its western horizon, I look with a more unwavering faith toward the land where there will be no night."   Two years later we find his social character even more clearly revealed.   "Conscious that I am unfitted for large assemblies, I do not care to join them, but I never loved the few who are dear to me more than I do now, and never enjoyed being with them more highly ; and while they do not tire of me, I cannot give up that enjoyment which is, next to one, the sweetest cup in life.   Nor do I hold that the closing years of life should all be given up to penitence and ascetic devotion.   Real religion is of another cast, its services are man's highest duties, and the proper performance of them contributes more to habitual cheerfulness than all the joys of earth.   Is there no devotion but in a monk's cell ? . . .   As regards reading,

I find there are few books of which I do *not* tire, and of these few the first of all is the Bible.   I have just finished a careful perusal of the four Gospels, having taken them up as if it were for the first time and I had never formed an opinion in regard to Him whose life they record, and in so far as I can divest myself of all preconceived belief.   I closed the book convinced by what I had been reading of the literal truth of the narrative, and saying with the centurion, ' Truly this was the Son of God.' "

AFTER-THOUGHTS.

IF the musician has his prelude, inter-
lude and postlude, certes the scribe may
be permitted his appendix. Comparatively few wills are executed without a
codicil ; and fewer still are the epistles,
especially those of the gentler sex, without the time-honored *postscript*. And in
social intercourse generally some words
at parting are deemed necessary, if they
do involve the somewhat saddening
phrase—farewell. George Selwyn on a
certain occasion, when in a courtly company, ventured the assertion that no
woman ever wrote a letter without adding to it a postscript. "My next shall
refute that statement," said Lady B.
In a few days Selwyn received a missive
from her ladyship, ending with the inevitable *P.S.* and the question, "*Now,
who was right, you or I?*"

So, if the courtesy of the reader has induced him to accompany the writer thus far, he will doubtless continue with him to the end of these closing sentences, for his patience will not, it is believed, be very severely taxed.

In conning over these brief studies of the eminent persons whose illustrious careers have been glanced at, many a suggestive hint of ethical teaching or inspiration may be garnered, and many a gem of poesy culled to charm the fancy. If, perchance, some portions may seem to savor too much of the homiletic, it is to be remembered that fidelity to the delineation of character required it ; and, moreover, life has its shadowy as well as its sunny aspects. Cultured intellect and moral elevation of character are the consummate blossom of a life of studious toil and self-discipline ; and these great elements imply solitude and soliloquy, as well as patient hours of quiescent thought. All great achievements have been thus engendered. In these unrestful times, when everything seems whirled along with such electric speed, who does not turn with relief from the " madd'ning world's ignoble strife" to the calm study of exalted character with its ethical and sagacious teaching ?

It has been well said that "some men of a secluded and studious life have sent forth from their closet or their cloister rays of intellectual light that have agitated courts and revolutionized kingdoms." Thus solitude becomes ofttimes the birthplace of important ideas and results. Sequestered from the strife of tongues and the ever-surging tide of human life, the student explores the mysteries and marvels of the great book of Nature, and solves her problems.

Thomas Fuller quaintly remarks that " some sciolists have discovered a short path to celebrity. Having heard that it is a vastly silly thing to believe everything, they take it for granted that it would be a vastly wise thing to believe nothing. They, therefore, set up for free-thinkers ; but their stock in trade is, that they are free *from* thinking. No persons make so large a demand against the reason of others as those who have none of their own ; as a highwayman will take greater liberties with our purse than our banker." Said Cowley, " I love and commend a true, good fame, because it is the shadow of virtue —not that it doth any good to the body which accompanies it, but it is an efficacious shadow, and, like that of St. Peter, cures the diseases of others." Mental, like muscular activity, is essential to healthy development ; the firefly emits its phosphorescent light only when a-wing, and the lark sings as he soars. Good and great men have been compared to the stars—the planets of the age, wherein they live and illustrate the times. Jeremy Collier has said that " intellectual pleasures are of a nobler kind than any others. They belong to beings of the highest order ; they are the inclinations of heaven and the entertainments of the Deity."

As the patent of nobility is theirs whose lives are found worthy and have been prolific of benefits to others, the symbol of esteem for the eminent characters who have so recently passed away should be on that account, rather than the laurel crown of old, a wreath of the more familiar, fragrant, many-hued beauties of Flora.